FROM THE WORLD OF Pε

REAL
YOUR GUIDE TO THE
DEMIGOD TRAINING CAMP

Disney • HYPERION
Los Angeles   New York

A special thank you to Stephanie True Peters
for her help with this book

Illustrations by Stef Masciandaro

Copyright © 2017 by Rick Riordan
All rights reserved. Published by Disney • Hyperion,
an imprint of Buena Vista Books, Inc. No part of this book may
be reproduced or transmitted in any form or by any means,
electronic or mechanical, including photocopying, recording, or
by any information storage and retrieval system, without written
permission from the publisher. For information address
Disney • Hyperion, 77 West 66th Street, New York, New York 10023.

First Hardcover Edition, May 2017
First Trade Paperback Edition, November 2023
1 3 5 7 9 10 8 6 4 2
FAC-004510-23271
Printed in the United States of America

This book is set in New Baskerville/Fontspring

Library of Congress Cataloging-in-Publication Control
Number for Hardcover Edition: 2016042145

ISBN 978-1-368-10083-0

Follow @Read Riordan
Visit www.DisneyBooks.com

To all campers, past and present

CONTENTS

Praise me, demigods!
I made you this helpful film.
Trust me. It's awesome.

—Haiku by Apollo introducing his orientation film
Welcome to Camp Half-Blood

Trust _me_. The film
was more awful than
awesome.
—P.J.

MOVIE NIGHT

by Percy Jackson

Hey, everybody. Percy Jackson here. You might know me as the guy who helped save the world from total destruction—twice, but who's counting? I like to think of myself as just another Greek demigod lucky enough to have found Camp Half-Blood.

If you can read this, then surprise! You're probably a demigod too. That's because only demigods—and a few special mortals, like my mom and Rachel Elizabeth Dare—can read what's actually written here. To everyone else, this book is called *The Complete History of Pavement* and it's about . . . well, that should be obvious. You can thank the Mist for that choice of topic.

So, demigod, chances are you're making your way to camp with your satyr guide. Or maybe you've already arrived and are reading this with the hope that it'll calm your nerves. I'd say there's a fifty-fifty chance of *that* happening.

But I'm getting off topic. (I do that. I have ADHD. Bet you know what that's like.) What I'm supposed to do is explain the story behind this book.

A few months ago, Chiron—he's the immortal centaur who's also our camp activities director—was called away to rescue two unclaimed demigods and their satyr guide. (The satyr had gotten himself into a sticky situation. It took him days to get his fur clean.) Anyway, Argus, our resident security guard and part-time chauffeur, drove Chiron on this mission because, well, can you imagine a centaur driving an SUV? (You can? Hmm. Maybe you're a child of Hypnos and saw it in a dream.) Our camp director, Mr. D (aka Dionysus, the god of wine), was MIA, so that left us demigods on our own.

"Don't destroy Half-Blood while we're gone," was Chiron's parting instruction. Argus pointed two fingers at his eyes and then at us. This took a few minutes since he has one hundred eyes, but we got the message—be good, or else.

We went about our usual routines—combat practice, volleyball practice, archery practice, strawberry-picking practice (don't ask), lava-wall-climbing practice. . . . You'll find we practice a lot here. We would have spent the evening in the usual way, too, with a campfire sing-along, if not for an off-hand comment Nico di Angelo dropped at dinner.

We were talking about what changes each of us would make if we ran the camp, and Nico said:

"First thing I'd do is make sure the poor newbie demigods don't have to suffer through the orientation film."

All conversation stopped. "What orientation film?" Will Solace asked.

Nico looked puzzled. "You know. . . ." He glanced side to side, clearly uncomfortable with everybody watching him. Finally he cleared his throat and sang in a warbly voice to the tune of "The Hokey Pokey": "It lets the demigods in! It shuts the monsters out! It keeps the half-bloods safe, but turns mortals all about! It's Misty, and it's magic, and it makes me want to shout: the border is all about!" He punctuated the last line of the song with some halfhearted claps.

We stared at him in stunned silence.

"Nico." Will patted his boyfriend's arm. "You're scaring the other campers."

"More than usual," Julia Feingold muttered under her breath.

"Oh, come on," Nico protested. "You've all heard that annoying song, right? It's from *Welcome to Camp Half-Blood.*"

Nobody responded.

"The orientation film," Nico added.

We shared a group shrug.

Nico groaned. "You mean I just sang in public and . . . I'm the only one who's ever seen that stupid film?"

"So far, anyway," said Connor Stoll. He leaned forward, a mischievous glint in his eyes. "Where, exactly, did you see this cinematic masterpiece?"

"Chiron's office in the Big House," Nico replied.

Connor pushed back from the table and stood up.

"Where are you going?" Will asked.

"Chiron's office in the Big House."

Annabeth Chase—my awesome girlfriend, a daughter of Athena—frowned suspiciously. "Connor . . . Chiron's office is locked."

"Is it?" Connor laced his fingers together and cracked his knuckles. "We'll see about that." He turned to Harley, the oddly muscular eight-year-old son of Hephaestus. "Want to come with? I might need help with the projector."

"A projectile! Yes!" Harley pumped his fist.

"A projector," Connor corrected. "And you can't make it do anything but show the movie. No exploding upgrades. No turning it into a killer robot."

"Aww . . ." Harley scowled in disappointment, but he followed Connor to the Big House.

I glanced at Nico. "Now look what you've started."

He snorted. "This is *my* fault? What do you want me to do—stop them?"

"Stop them?" I grinned. "Nah, man. I think we should get some popcorn ready."

An hour later, we gathered in the amphitheater to watch *Welcome to Camp Half-Blood*. Connor and Harley had successfully set up the screen and projector without any killer-robot-exploding mishaps, which I appreciated. I figured the movie would be a typical orientation flick—a monotone voiceover; a tour of the campgrounds; happy demigods going about their business, trying to pretend the cameras didn't exist. Then the opening credits rolled.

"Uh-oh," Will muttered. "This is going to be . . . interesting."

It turned out the creative genius behind the movie was Will's dad—the god Apollo, which meant this was *not* going to be a typical orientation flick. No, as we soon found out, Apollo had written, directed, produced, hosted, and starred in . . . *a variety show.*

For those of you who don't know what a variety show is, imagine a talent show on steroids, complete with canned laughter, prerecorded applause, and an extra-large helping of hokeyness. For the next hour, we cringe-watched as Apollo and our demigod pre-decessors performed in song-and-dance numbers, recited poetry, acted in comedy sketches, and harmonized in a musical group called the Lyre Choir. Naturally, Apollo featured prominently in most of the acts. The one of him Hula-Hooping shirtless while satyrs capered around with long rainbow ribbons on sticks . . . you can't unsee that kind of thing. I'm seriously considering asking Hera to purge it from my memory.

(Okay, not really. I am not going through *that* again.)

Still, I get what Apollo was going for. Each number highlighted something important about Camp Half-Blood—the cabins, the training arenas, the Big House, et cetera, et cetera. The trouble is, Apollo didn't seem to know much about the camp. According to Valentina Diaz's assessment of the hairstyles and fashions, the movie dated from the 1950s, so maybe the film accurately depicted what Camp Half-Blood was like back then. If so, yikes. Take it from me: a *lot* has changed in sixty years.

That's where *Camp Half-Blood Confidential* comes in. After seeing Apollo's film, we decided we *really* had to take action. We needed to offer our incoming demigods something better for orientation. And so—*BOOM.* You hold in your hands the definitive guide to life here at our beloved Greek demigod training facility. It's written for demigods by demigods, which means you get the inside, behind-the-scenes scoop on just about everything. You'll get the lay of the land, too, thanks to descriptions of sites written by Pete, a geyser god with a flair for selling it like it is. Oh, the stories we'll tell and the secrets you'll learn . . . though I promise you, I will *not* sing and dance with a Hula-Hoop.

One last thing: we wouldn't dream of completely depriving you of the *Welcome to Camp Half-Blood* movie experience. So we've included some choice excerpts from the film throughout the book—annotated by yours truly. Enjoy the show! (Cue maniacal laughter.)

SCENE: Darkness. Suddenly, a single spotlight illuminates Apollo standing on the front porch of the Big House. The house is a bold red color, a stark contrast to the short white chiton Apollo wears. He clears his throat and speaks.

APOLLO: A poem by Apollo, recited dramatically by . . . Apollo:
O, Immortal Chiron,
Centaur wise and true,
Trainer of our heroes,
Just remember who taught you.
—The opening scene of *Welcome to Camp Half-Blood*

Apollo's chiton was so short, I held my breath throughout this scene, praying he didn't bend over.
-P.J.

THREE (FOUR?) THOUSAND YEARS AND COUNTING

by Chiron

I was just a young centaur, living alone in a cave on Mount Pelion, when I first met Lord Apollo. He literally dropped in out of the sky, which nearly gave me a heart attack. It wasn't every day an A-list divinity with perfect teeth and glowing golden robes appeared on my hillside.

"You're Kronos's son, right?" Apollo pulled up a boulder and sat down. "My dad is Zeus! He's Kronos's son too. So I guess that makes you my uncle. How weird is that?"

"Ah . . . yes, Lord Apollo." I tried to control the twitching in my withers. "Very weird indeed." I noticed the sky was darkening even though it was only noon. "Not to be critical, O Great One, but shouldn't you be driving the sun chariot right now?"

He shrugged. "Actually, I put it in park for a few minutes because Artemis is up there doing her lunar-eclipse thing." He scratched his fashionably stubbled chin. "Or is it solar? I can never keep them straight." Suddenly he jumped from his boulder as if he'd had a marvelous idea. "But that's not important! I remember what I came down here to ask you. I've never ridden a centaur before. Mind taking me for a spin around the block?"

"Um . . ."

He put his fingers to his temples and intoned, "I predict you're going to say yes."

FYI, centaurs hate being taken for a ride, either literally or metaphorically. Nevertheless, I managed a forced smile. "I would be . . . delighted. Yes."

"Oh, yeah!" Apollo crowed triumphantly. "Who has two thumbs and the gift of prophecy?" He jerked his thumbs at himself. "This god!"

As it turned out, giving Apollo a centaur-back ride was the smartest thing I ever did. Unlike others of my kind, I didn't belong to a specific tribe. I was a loner . . . and, sometimes, lonely. We bonded during that ride. I found that Apollo could be quite charming one-on-one, when he wasn't trying to impress his adoring throngs of fans. When we got back to the cave, he said something that changed my life.

"Uncle Chiron, I've decided to teach you some stuff."

Perhaps he found the idea amusing: a nephew

teaching his uncle. Or maybe, being the god of prophecy, he suspected I had an important role to play in the future of Olympus. Whatever the reason, he chose to share his knowledge with me.

At first, he showed me simple things, like how to nock an arrow—"Aim the pointy end *away* from your body"—and how to bandage a gushing battle wound. He taught me to make a lyre, play a number of hits like "Stairway to Olympus" and "Burnt-Offering Smoke on the Water," and even compose my own lyrics. Once, in an effort to refine my poetry skills, he sent me on a quest to find a rhyme for *arugula* so that he could finish an ode to a mixed-green salad. The best I could do was *pergola*. Apollo called my effort an "ode fail"—the ancient precursor to today's "epic fail"—but he continued to work with me.

The lessons went on for a year. Then one day, Apollo showed up at the doorway of my cave with a half-dozen young demigods. "You know all that stuff I taught you?" he asked me. "It's time to pay it forward! I'd like you to meet Achilles, Aeneas, Jason, Atalanta, Asclepius, and Percy—"

"It's Perseus, sir," said one of the young men.

"Whatever!" Apollo grinned with delight.

"Chiron, teach them everything I showed you. Y'all have fun!" Then he vanished.

I turned to the youngsters. They frowned at me. The one named Achilles drew his sword.

"Apollo expects us to learn from a centaur?" he demanded. "Centaurs are wild barbarians, worse than the Trojans!"

"Hey, shut up," said Aeneas.

"Gentlemen and lady," I interceded. "I assure you I am a different sort of centaur. Allow me to teach you, and I promise I will not make you participate in any crude centaur behavior like butting heads to the death or wearing drink helmets."

Atalanta looked a little disappointed. "Butting heads to the death sounds fun . . . but I guess I can give your teachings a try."

We got down to business.

First, I assessed their combat skills. Aeneas performed surprisingly well for a son of Aphrodite; I expected him to be a lover, not a fighter, and yet he actually knew how to use his sword as a sword rather than as a fashion accessory. The other demigods had some work to do. Atalanta seemed to think all training matches had to be fought to the death. She also referred to her classmates as *dirty, stupid men*, which made team-building difficult. Achilles spent his entire time in combat defending his right heel, an unusual maneuver that baffled me until I found out about his childhood dip in the River Styx. I tried to tell the boy to wear ironshod boots rather than sandals, but he simply wouldn't listen. As for Asclepius, in one-on-one melees he had an off-putting habit of darting in and feeling his opponent's forehead for signs of fever.

Next I tested my pupils for ingenuity. I handed out random materials and instructed them to improvise potentially lifesaving objects. "This ancient skill is known as *MacGyvering*," I told them. Sadly, none of my inaugural group of students was a child of Hephaestus, so no one did very well with this assignment. When I hinted to Perseus that he could hammer and polish his Celestial bronze to make a mirrored shield, he rolled his eyes and scoffed, "What would I ever use *that* for?"

Likewise, most failed miserably with musical composition. Only Jason came up with something memorable: a mesmerizing *stomp-stomp CLAP* rhythm that so stirred the blood we adopted it as our pre-battle beat. (You can still hear that *stomp-stomp CLAP* rhythm pounded out at athletic competitions today, along with the chant "We will, we will . . . ROCK YOU!")

It was clear that the demigods had a lot to learn. But I didn't mind. As we sang together by the campfire that first night, I felt as if I finally had a tribe of my own.

I taught the six demigods everything I knew. Then I sent them out into the world, where they fulfilled their destinies as heroes. Triple-threat Atalanta earned fame as a fleet-footed sprinter, a sure-shot huntress, and the only female Argonaut. Jason and his crew sailed into legend by securing the Golden Fleece and impressing the populace with myriad seafaring adventures. Achilles and Aeneas became mighty warriors—though, sadly, they fought on opposite sides in the Trojan War. (Spoiler alert: Achilles and Greece won, but Achilles was killed when he forgot to defend his heel.) Perseus discovered that a mirrored shield was useful after all when he faced a certain snake-headed gorgon, and as for Asclepius, he became the greatest medical mind in ancient history. Their heroic deeds live on in the memories of mortals to this day.

So I must have done something right.

More demigods regularly arrived at Mount Pelion, and I trained them all. Word of my success spread. When my cave was no longer large enough, I built a one-of-a-kind full-immersion training facility in the foothills of Mount Olympus. I named it Camp Half-Blood because it was dedicated to training the half-divine children of mortals and deities. I also opened the doors to many other species, such as satyrs, pegasi, and harpies.

The satyrs arrived en masse with this note from Apollo:

I predict that in the future, demigods won't be able to find Camp Half-Blood on their own. The world will simply be too large, too populous, and too dangerous. When that time comes, send satyrs to track down your prospective students. Satyrs can find anything. They recently located a herd of cattle Hermes stole from me that even I couldn't find. Trust me: you need seekers, and they're the goats for the job.

The first Camp Half-Blood was modest—just an open-air arena for combat practice, a courtyard for meetings and dining, and a large stone building with sleeping quarters. The building made an impression on at least one camper, who exclaimed, "Now *that's* a big house!" when she saw it. The name stuck, and forever after our headquarters has been called the Big House.

The demigods lived together in the Big House at first, but with more campers coming each year, space became tight. Fights broke out. Demigods, it seemed, inherited rivalries as well as gifts from their godly parents. To keep the peace, I divided them into family groups and told them to design and build cabins that honored their godly parents. Thankfully, the bickering died down to a quiet roar after that.

As Apollo had once turned over teaching duties to me, I turned over some of the training to experienced campers. I meant for them to pass along their knowledge of fighting and survival skills. And they did, but they also passed along family feuds, closely guarded secrets, and hazing traditions. When the Hephaestus cabin almost burned down the dryads' forest during a late-night game of truth or dare ("Dare: blow up this amphora"), I asked Argus the Hundred-Eyed to join our staff as security guard.

At the time, Argus was recovering from a near-death experience. On Hera's orders, Hermes had brained him with a rock while Argus was guarding a white heifer—who was actually Io, Zeus's latest, er, lady friend. Hera saved Argus by turning him into a peacock. He eventually morphed back into his original form and jumped at the chance to come to Camp Half-Blood. Good thing he did, too, for without him, we might not have detected the first major threat to our existence: a monstrous horde that almost wiped Camp Half-Blood off the map.

"Whole bunch coming," Argus reported late one night. "Nasty ones." (Even back then, he didn't waste words. Having an eye in the middle of your tongue makes talking uncomfortable, not to mention eating hot soup.)

We'd had random monster attacks before. We'd always fended them off. But this attack was different. It was an organized effort—I never discovered who organized it, though I have my suspicions—and it was *huge.*

Hundreds of monsters—nasty ones indeed—swarmed the camp from every corner. I sounded the conch horn to raise the alarm, grabbed my bow and quiver, and galloped into the courtyard. "This is not a drill, people!" I cried. Demigods surged out of their cabins to face the greatest challenge of their young lives. Win, and Camp Half-Blood would endure. Lose, and the camp, along with countless lives, would be lost forever.

Fighting raged through the night. The demigods battled bravely and with skill, destroying monsters with swords, spears, arrows, and other weapons. But we were far outnumbered. I feared Camp Half-Blood was doomed.

Then, just as rosy-fingered dawn peeked over the horizon, a new battle cry sounded in the distance. Former campers who had learned of our desperate plight now came charging to our aid. As one, we attacked our enemies with renewed vigor. We cut down one monster after another until their dusty remains blanketed the ground. Those we didn't send to Tartarus fled back into the wilds.

I had never been prouder of my campers, old and new. Nor had I ever been more ashamed of myself.

You see, I knew that so many demigods living in one place was like an all-you-can-kill buffet for monsters. Yet I had convinced myself that our campers needed no other protection than the skills we taught them. My pride had nearly been our destruction, but I learned my lesson. I immediately sent an Iris-message to Olympus asking for help. The gods heard our plea. The next day, a magical border settled over and around the grounds—a barrier that would both conceal the camp from unfriendly eyes and repel future attacks.

The camp has changed locations over the millennia, always grounding itself near the seat of Olympus as the gods move from one dominant nation to another. Thousands of demigods have called Camp Half-Blood home since that long-ago battle. You might know some of their names: Arthur. Merlin. Guinevere. Charlemagne. Joan of Arc. Napoleon. George Washington. Harriet Tubman. Madame Curie. Frank Lloyd Wright. Amelia Earhart. And many more demigods, still living, who have asked that I not reveal their identities. New names are added to the list each summer, and more still will join the ranks in the centuries ahead.

That is my hope, at least. For the demigods of the past, present, and future are more than just campers to me. They make my immortal life worth living. They are my tribe.

CREATURE
COMFORTS

SCENE: A background choir of demigod a cappella singers stands on stage. They're dressed in classic 1950s doo-wop attire—black suits, white shirts, skinny ties. Apollo, similarly attired except that his tie is gold, takes center stage. He faces the singers and strums a chord on his lyre. He points to the boys.

BOYS [singing]: *Dooooooooooo!*

[Apollo points to the girls]

GIRLS [harmonizing]: *Waaaaaaaaaaa!*

[Apollo points to himself]

APOLLO [spit-singing]: *Ppppppppp!*

[Apollo waves his arm]

ALL: *Dooo-waaapppp!*

APOLLO: Ladies and gentlemen . . . the Lyre Choir!

[Applause]

BOYS and GIRLS [singing soft background harmony with a slow beat]: *Doo-da-doo, waa, waa. Doo-da-doo, waa, waa.* [continues]

APOLLO [crooning to the beat]: *Marble may be marble-lous,*
And wood might be good.
Stone's a sturdy choice

For this half-blood neighborhood.
But for my children's cabin,
I demand something more divine.
So give me precious metal,
[background harmony swells]
And make it GOLD every time!
ALL: *Gold, gold, gold, gold—there's nothing quite so bright!*
Gold, gold, gold, gold—it reflects Apollo's might!
[Apollo cuts off background singers]
APOLLO [crooning solo]: *Silver suits my sister*
But unattended, it can tarnish.
Roofs of thatch are fine, I guess,
But why not add some varnish?
[background harmony resumes softly]
Vines of wine are creepy,
And abalone smells of fish.
[background harmony grows louder]
Red's too strong a color,
And gray is boring-ish.
[background harmony grows louder still]
That's why my children's cabin
Is made of something more divine.
I'm worth that precious metal—
[background harmony swells]

So make it GOLD every time!

[Cheers and applause]

ALL: *Gold, gold, gold, gold . . .*

For the record, my cabin's abalone walls do NOT smell of fish.
—P.J.

THE DIVINE CABINS

Talk about curb appeal! Tastefully decorated inside and out, these charming units are big on comfort and totally unique in style—one might even say each has its own personality! Of course, location is key, and you couldn't ask for a better spot than this. The twenty cabins are within easy walking distance of all camp amenities as well as training and recreational facilities. Don't see a unit dedicated to your particular godly parent? No worries! Once you're claimed, one can be built to suit. In the meantime, pull up a bunk in Cabin Eleven and stay awhile!

> **WARNING!** The divine cabins area is an active construction site, so please watch out for exposed nails, exploding blocks, and cracks that could plummet you to the Underworld.

SPACE COULD BE AN ISSUE

by Annabeth Chase

For generations, Camp Half-Blood had only twelve cabins—one for each major Olympian deity. The odd-numbered cabins were dedicated to the Olympic gods, the even ones to the Olympic goddesses—except for Cabin Twelve, which Dionysus took over when Hestia gave him her seat on the Council of Olympus, but that's another story. Anyway, after the Titan War, my kindhearted boyfriend, Percy, made the Olympians promise that *all* demigods, not just the kids of the major twelve, would have cabins of their own.

Which is just like Percy: doing something impulsive and compassionate, and making my life difficult in the process. See, I'm the camp's resident architect, which meant that the task of designing all those new cabins fell to me.

Don't get me wrong. I supported Percy's plan one hundred percent. But after building units thirteen through sixteen—Hades, Iris, Hypnos, and Nemesis—the cabin area started to look cramped. I met with Chiron to discuss the problem.

"Space," I told him, "could be an issue."

"Any ideas?" Chiron asked.

I brainstormed aloud: "We build upward, combine new cabins into one tall complex. Demigods associated with the earth on lower levels, with the sky on top."

Chiron shook his head. "Intriguing idea, but experience has shown me that demigods from different families don't cohabitate well."

"Okay, scratch that." I pointed at the nearby forest. "What about tree houses? Enclosed platforms, elevated walkways, ladders, rope swings—"

Chiron cut me off. "The dryads wouldn't go for it. And imagine what would happen if a demigod took to sleepwalking."

"Caves?"

"Only one available, and Apollo has claimed it for his Oracle."

"Houseboats?"

"Sleepwalking again, plus the naiads would nix it. Also, we need the lake for trireme practice."

I cast around for inspiration. My eyes fixed on Hestia, who was tending her hearth in the center of the commons. You'd think a major Olympian goddess would attract a lot of notice sitting in the middle of camp, but Hestia came and went without any fanfare, usually in the shape of a young girl in plain brown robes. I hadn't noticed her, because she was so small and low profile.

Small and low profile.

An idea hit me like a Zeus-thrown thunderbolt.

"I'll get back to you tomorrow," I told Chiron.

The old centaur chuckled. "I know that look. You have an idea."

"Yeah," I admitted. In fact, my brain was buzzing. "But I want to work out some details before I share it with you. See you at breakfast."

That night I worked into the wee hours, pausing only to . . . well, to wee. In the morning I had my blueprints ready, but I still needed more time.

At breakfast, I broke the news to Chiron. "I want to set up a construction site in the southern woods."

He furrowed his bushy eyebrows. "You're not thinking of building the cabins there, are you? As I said, the dryads won't—"

"I just need a secluded work area," I said. "I won't build anything big or permanent in that space. Trust me on this, okay?"

Chiron stroked his beard. "Well, you've never let me down before. And I do owe you for designing those centaur-size bathrooms for the Big House. Very well, Annabeth. You have my permission."

The next days were a feverish blur of measuring, sawing, and hammering. By week's end, I'd completed a full-scale model of my design, premounted on a wheeled platform for easy moving. I bribed my pegasus friends Blackjack and Porkpie with some donuts, and they agreed to haul my creation out of the woods and into the commons.

A few campers wandered over to see what I'd built. "It's supercute!" gushed Lacy from the Aphrodite cabin. "But what is it?"

"A portable storage shed," Clarisse La Rue guessed, eyeing the wheels. "Or a covered chariot. No, wait. It's a rapid-deployment outhouse."

"None of the above," I replied, slightly offended. "I call it a tiny house. Check it out!"

I threw open the door and invited them in, a few at a time. The main sitting room was compact but perfectly livable. Two built-in cushioned benches along the walls doubled as beds. I lifted the cushions.

"And see? There's storage underneath the beds for your clothes, armor, weapons. It's even long enough for that electric spear of yours, Clarisse."

"Uh-huh."

Clarisse sounded unimpressed, but that didn't dampen my enthusiasm. I pointed to the narrow staircase against the back wall. "Upstairs is a loft with two more twin beds. Or it could be used as a game room, meeting area, whatever. I made the ceiling extra high so headroom isn't an issue. Under the stairs is more built-in storage. But the best part is over here."

I squeezed past them and rolled open a narrow pocket door in the corner. "Ta-da!"

"So it *is* an outhouse," Clarisse said.

"It's a private bathroom," I corrected. "Whoever lives here never has to use the common facilities again." I smirked at her, remembering the drenching Percy had once given her by blowing up the camp toilets. "You of all people should appreciate *that*."

Clarisse reddened. "I'm coming down with claustrophobia." She shoved past me and out the door.

I turned to Lacy. "You see the potential here, right? Microhouses are the future. This is cutting-edge architecture!"

She looked at the whitewashed walls, taupe cushions, and unadorned windows. "Well, it's kind of . . . boring inside."

"It's only the model," I said defensively. "Whoever lives here can decorate it however—"

A tap on the door interrupted me. Chiron poked his head in and frowned. "I would come in for a tour, but, ah, I fear there is no room."

"Good luck," Lacy whispered to me. Then she slipped past Chiron and hurried away.

I got out of the way so Chiron could come in and clop around the tiny house. It was large enough to accommodate him, but just barely. The entire walk-through took him about three steps.

When he emerged again, he looked deep in thought.

"It's only the model," I told him.

"Hmm?" He focused on me as if trying to process my words. Then he exhaled with relief. "Oh, a *model*. I see. In that case . . . yes, this might work." He scanned the cabin area as if calculating the acreage. "We'll need about four, don't you think? Please proceed with construction."

Designing and building one tiny house had been

fun. Constructing four? I was over the moon. "I won't let you down, Chiron!"

Two weeks later, I let him down.

I had been working overtime to modify my original design. I widened the doorways for better access. I got some magical paint from the Hephaestus cabin so the exterior color of each new minibuilding could be changed with just a touch, making each one unique. I applied everything I knew about extra-dimensional construction to create impossibly deep storage containers, a larger shower in the bathroom, and built-in furniture that could be moved, collapsed, or reshaped as desired. With a snap of your fingers, you could turn the living area into a bedroom, or a gym, or a dining room, or a military command center that even Clarisse would be proud of. I added a dozen preprogrammed interior-decorating schemes so Lacy could never accuse the space of being boring. When I finally rolled out the new cabins and proudly presented them to Chiron, I expected him to be pleased. Instead, he looked puzzled.

"Um . . . is this it?"

I frowned. "You asked for four, right?"

"Four *cabins*. Not four *models*."

My spirits deflated like a bunch of month-old party balloons.

"Oh, dear," Chiron murmured when he saw my face. "That model you showed me—that was the *full-size* cabin, wasn't it?"

I nodded. "That was the whole point, wasn't it? Saving space? I—I thought smaller buildings . . ."

He kindly laid his hand on my shoulder. "Annabeth, your work is exemplary. But as lovely as these units are, I fear that the children of, ah, *lesser* deities—for lack of a better term—will not appreciate accommodations so much smaller than the other cabins."

The flaw in my concept was so obvious, I couldn't believe I hadn't considered it. The whole point of Percy's plan was so our new recruits—and their godly parents—would feel included at camp—equal, not *lesser*. But they wouldn't see my tiny houses as fun minimalist living spaces. They'd see them as yet another snub from the more powerful deities and their kids. I was so embarrassed, I wanted to crawl under a rock.

"I'll get Harley to blow up the tiny houses," I mumbled. "He'll like that." I turned to go, but Chiron stopped me.

"Wait a moment." He studied the units. "These have wheels."

"Yeah. I mean, they don't *have* to have wheels, but I thought—"

"Perhaps I was too hasty," Chiron said. "Let me try something."

He put his shoulder to the closest minicabin and pushed it toward the next one in line. Having the strength of a stallion, Chiron had no trouble moving the tiny houses around. A few more shoves and he had arranged the four units so they were back-to-back, two on either side. The slanted rooftops joined into one centerline peak. In short, the tiny houses looked as if they'd been designed to fit together as a single structure that was about the same size as the older cabins.

"You know," Chiron said, "I think this might work quite nicely for our newest pair of demigods." He called across the commons, "Holly! Laurel!"

Identical twin girls who had been arguing on the steps of Hermes cabin raced over, each trying to push the other out of the way so she could be first.

"What's up?" asked the one on the left.

"Contest?" the one on the right asked eagerly. "World war?"

"Something even more exciting," Chiron promised. "Annabeth, I'd like you to meet Laurel and Holly Victor, recently claimed daughters of Nike, the goddess of victory. Laurel, Holly, this is Annabeth Chase, the most gifted architect at camp. She redesigned the palaces of Mount Olympus!"

The twins' eyes widened in amazement. I felt a little self-conscious with Chiron praising me. I was, in fact, the *only* architect at camp. But that bit about redesigning Mount Olympus—that was true. It was the centerpiece of my college-admissions portfolio.

"What you see in front of you," Chiron continued, "is Annabeth's latest triumph: completely customizable, modular cabins."

Laurel edged toward the nearest tiny house. She peeked inside the door. "It's small."

"Ah, but it's not!" Chiron said. "It's *private*. Each module is for a maximum of four people. How many do you have to live with right now in the Hermes cabin?"

"Like a thousand," Holly grumbled. "All losers, too."

I didn't think the Hermes kids would appreciate that, but I understood what Chiron was trying to do. I chimed in. "These modules are *brand-new*. The bathrooms are state-of-the-art."

Laurel's eyes lit up. "Bathrooms *in* the cabin?"

"Yep," I said. "The furniture is programmable. The exterior colors, the interior design—it can be changed to whatever you want." I touched the nearest cabin, willing it to turn from dull red to bright silver.

"Whoa," said Holly.

"But we can't give brand-new cabins like this to just anyone," I said. "Whoever gets these, everyone else in camp will be totally jealous. We need to find the absolute best campers—"

"Us," Holly said. "Obviously."

"Me," Laurel corrected her sister. "With you a distant second."

"So who wants to claim a bunk first?"

"Me!" the sisters yelled simultaneously. They charged to the same front door, growling as they tried to push each other out of the way. Then they split apart and made for different entrances.

Shouts rang out from inside the cabins.

"I'll get to my loft before you!" one sister cried.

"Ha! No chance, loser! I'm already halfway up!"

Chiron turned toward me and smiled. "There

we are. Modular units that can be rearranged and moved as desired! Each cluster can be as big or small as we need it to be. More campers can be fit into the same amount of space as a regular cabin, but with more privacy and better accommodations. Annabeth Chase, you are a genius!"

I listened to the sounds of pounding footsteps and triumphant crowing from the Victor sisters as they argued about whose module was the coolest.

"Thanks," I told Chiron. "Genius was exactly what I was going for."

My tiny-house mash-up brought the cabin count to seventeen. Three more units—Hebe, Tyche, and Hecate—were added afterward, and construction crews are ready to build more. Space might still be an issue someday, depending on how many gods we end up needing to represent, but you know what? Not one person has complained about my tiny houses being too tiny. In fact, when I get out of college, I may go into business designing portable microhousing for demigods. It beats building rapid-response out-houses, at least.

THE BIG HOUSE

Brought to you by Pete the Palikos

This four-story sky-blue Victorian is a bona fide gem. The vast wraparound porch offers ample space for pinochle players and convalescents alike. The basement is currently set up for strawberry-jam storage, but can also be used to hide the occasional demigod driven insane by the Labyrinth. The first-floor living quarters, camp infirmary, and combination rec room / meeting room are wheelchair accessible, as is a specially designed bronze-lined office. The rooms of the top floors stand ready to welcome overnight guests, while the attic, now free of its resident desiccated mummy, provides the perfect catchall for camper discards and memorabilia.

TONGS A LOT, DAD

by Connor Stoll

People think I'm a thief, a sneak, a pickpocket, and a lock picker. They're right, of course, but c'mon—how else am I supposed to spend my time while waiting for a quest?

When my brother, Travis, was here (he's in college now), we explored every inch of camp except one area: the Big House attic. No way either of us was setting foot in there while that ol' leather-skinned hippie Oracle was propped in the corner.

But then Spooky gave up the spirit and crumbled to dust on the Big House front porch. We saw our chance and took it. While everyone else was waiting to see if Rachel, the new Oracle, would survive the spirit invasion (spoiler: she did), we made our move around to the back door of the Big House.

It was locked. (Ha!) One pick, three clicks, and *BOOM!*—we were inside. Thanks to past reconnaissance missions, we knew the way up to the attic. We pulled down the stairs and stuck our heads through the trapdoor and into a thieves' paradise.

We ignored the junk, like that old three-legged

stool the mummy used to sit on. But other pieces seemed to scream *Pick me! Pick me!* as if itching to be freed from their dusty attic prison. That glittery crown on the mannequin in the far corner. That emerald-pommeled sword hanging on the wall. That *sweet* Elvis-style rhinestone cape, which for some reason was draped across the shoulders of a stuffed taxidermic grizzly bear.

Travis and I had planned to take our time and really search through the stuff. But then, for no apparent reason, this beam of golden light shot upward through the floor and engulfed the Oracle's old three-legged stool. The light shut off as quickly as it had appeared, and the stool was gone. I didn't know what had just happened. Maybe Apollo was teleporting the stool to its new owner. Maybe somebody was randomly blasting disintegrator rays in our direction. Hey, you never know what those Hephaestus kids will do. Anyway, it kind of freaked us out. We decided not to stick around, just in case that weird beam came back and zapped us away too. We grabbed the nearest things we could reach—a canvas sack for me, a small wooden box for Travis—and got out of that attic faster than you can say Hermes Express.

Back at our cabin, we chased the other demigods

outside and told them to go play in the woods or something (being co–head counselors does have its privileges). Then we sat down to examine our take.

Travis opened the lid of his box. His eyes grew wide. "Whoa. It's a mystical bag of winds."

My pulse started to race. "Like the thermos Dad gave Percy that time? I've always wanted one of those! Let me see!"

All slow and dramatic, he pulled out a flat pink rubber sack with a thin nozzle at one end. "Behold!"

I smacked him on the arm. "That's a whoopee cushion, you idiot."

He burst out laughing. "Yeah, but I had you there for a second. Okay, your turn."

I rummaged in my bag and pulled out . . . a pair of barbecue tongs.

Travis snickered. "What are you going to do with those? You can't even toast bread without burning it. Are those things Celestial bronze at least?"

"Dunno. But there's an inscription: 'For plucking the Tartarus napkin from the fire.'" I turned them over and read the other side. "'One use only.'" I looked at Travis. "What the gods does that mean?"

"Well, Connor," my brother said, "I believe it means that you only get to use them once."

"Shut up." I almost threw my new tongs at him, then thought better of it. For some reason, that "Tartarus napkin" thing made me edgy. I decided to keep the tongs on me at all times—at least until I got my one use out of them.

Good thing I did, too, because later that summer, a napkin from Tartarus *did* appear in the dining pavilion fire. It's a long story, but if I hadn't had those tongs . . . well, I'm not sure I'd be writing this right now.

As for Travis, he loved his whoopee cushion so much he slept with it at night. At least, he claimed those sounds I heard were coming from the whoopee cushion. I kind of feel sorry for his college roommate.

THE DINING PAVILION

With its Greek marble columns and unencumbered views of the sky above, this inviting seaside facility screams classical elegance. The oversize tables, each reserved for members of a specific cabin, can easily accommodate up to twenty campers. The white tablecloths, edged with purple, add a dash of distinction. The menu boasts every food imaginable, and dishes are served and cleared by the loveliest dryads in the forest. Just don't forget to start your meal with a burnt offering to the gods! Oh, and ignore that crack in the marble floor—it's from a slight mishap when zombies were accidentally summoned from the Underworld. Nothing to worry about!

DINING PAVILION
ANNOUNCEMENTS

REMINDER:

Hecate head counselor Lou Ellen Blackstone and Hermes head counselors Travis and Connor Stoll will conduct cabin inspections this morning. Veteran campers, please assist your new cabinmates. As always, cleanest cabin wins first-shower privileges; filthiest cabin will clean the pegasus stables.

That is all.

UPDATE:

It has come to my attention that in the course of today's cabin inspections, several personal items went missing. Stoll brothers, please report to the Big House immediately.

That is all.

UPDATE:

You may recall that during today's cabin inspections, several personal items appeared to have gone missing. I say *appeared* because in fact, Lou Ellen hid the items by manipulating the Mist. Please see her for further details concerning the eventual reappearance of your possessions. Hermes cabin, my apologies.

Hecate cabin, please report to the pegasus stables. Blackjack and Porkpie are waiting.

That is all.

THE AMPHITHEATER

Just a stone's throw from the divine cabins, the Big House, and Half-Blood Hill, this gathering spot features rising tiers of stone bench seating that curve around the central stage. The benches are as comfortable as any mortal movie-theater chair, and there's not a bad view in the house. So take a seat, bask in the glow of the campfire, and add your voice to the joyful sing-along with such favorite hits as "Grandma Was a Gorgon" and "This Is Not Kumbaya; This Is Sparta!"

THE CAMP STORE

Brought to you by Pete the Palikos

Tragedy! You finally make it to camp alive—only to discover that you forgot your toothbrush! You could Iris-message your mortal parent for a new one. But do you really want to walk around with drakon breath until it arrives? Instead, hit the camp store! While you're there, be sure to check out the latest line of wind chimes—available in Celestial bronze, silver, and seashell—perfect for interpreting the voices of prophecy-spouting trees! If hanging bling in branches isn't your thing, how about the new Mythomagic expansion pack, Dual Deity Duel? The cards feature holographic images that change the gods' aspects from Greek to Roman and back. He's Ares! No, he's Mars! No, he's Ares again! Hours of dizzying head-to-head play! From tees to totes, whatever your needs, the camp store is your perfect one-stop shop.

TAKING INVENTORY

by Valentina Diaz

OMG, I just about *died* when I saw Apollo's orientation film. Those cute boys with their shorty-short swim trunks . . . um, yes, please!

As a daughter of Aphrodite, I'm always on the lookout for fresh "old-is-new" fashion ideas. Seeing those 1950s retro styles reminded me of a locked chest marked VINTAGE CLOTHING that I'd spotted in the back of the camp store a couple of days before. I'd been meaning to check out that chest, but Connor would never let me behind the counter to rummage through it. He was *so* annoying. He didn't understand the concept of browsing, like, *at all.*

Inspired by the film, I decided to take matters into my own hands. (Despite the fact that I'd just had a manicure.) I thought I might find some ideas for a new clothing line inside that trunk, so off I went!

Once inside the shop, I smashed open the lock on the trunk (Connor wasn't around). I was afraid I might just find musty retro T-shirts, knee-high tube socks (shudder!), skinny ties, and other stuff that dated back to the last century. But the clothing I found went way, *way* back; I'm talking, like, *millennia* back. Shows you what cedar lining and sachets of potpourri can do to keep clothes fresh, am I right?

The first thing that hit me about the vintage clothing was the colors. Red, yellow, green, blue, indigo: it was like Iris had thrown up on them—in, you know, a good way. I was stunned, because I'd always imagined the ancient Greeks dressed in white. I mean, that's what the clothing on the marble statues looks like, right? Then I remembered something Chiron had told me one time: the statues used to be painted, and they're white now only because the paint's worn off. Looking at the clothes in the trunk, I realized the ancient Greeks actually *had* worn colorful clothes. It made me proud of my ancestors.

I recognized the styles right away. On top were chitons—tuniclike thingies that were dress-length for women, thigh length for men, and (giggle) supershort for male athletes. Underneath were some himations, or cloaks, and a few peploses. A peplos is a big rectangle of fabric that could be turned into just about anything—kind of like those cute beach coverups that convert from shoulder wrap to halter-top dress to sleeveless dress to wraparound skirt. (Perfect for the budget-conscious shopper, BTW.) There were so many garments, I was afraid I'd miss something, so I grabbed a bunch of clothes hangers and racked those bad boys up.

"Oh, yeah." I ran my hand over the linen and wool. "It's dress-up time."

For the next hour, I tried on everything (except the *strophion*—it was too much like a tube top, which no girl should ever wear, in my opinion). I borrowed ancient Greek-style jewelry and footwear from the store's many storage lockers to complete my outfits. I was just twisting up my hair in an elaborate braided 'do when I saw one last item in the bottom of the trunk—an item I was pretty sure hadn't been there when I looked before.

"Holy Aphrodite's girdle!" I yelped as I pulled out . . . Aphrodite's girdle.

My hands trembled. I knew all about this particular article of clothing, though I'd never seen it in person before. Aphrodite was *super*-careful about when she wore it. Crafted for Mom by Hephaestus (when they were still on good speaking terms), the girdle was more like a fashionable belt—a finely wrought wide band of gold filigree (twenty karat, if I'm not mistaken)—infused with magic. Supposedly, anyone who saw Mom wearing it got whipped up in a frenzy of passion for her. Not that she needs any help in that department. I mean, everyone who sees her gets the hots for her.

As I held the magical belt, I couldn't help wondering if its power would work for me. I thought about taking it for a test drive around camp. I'd saunter past a certain Brazilian boy's cabin and pause long enough for him to take a gander. . . .

Tempting, I thought. But no.

I tossed the girdle back in the trunk. Why? Because I'd heard tales of Hephaestus cursing the items he made. The girdle probably wasn't cursed, but I wasn't going to chance triggering some dormant spell. Besides, any magic item used by the gods could be too much for demigods to handle.

As far as I know, the girdle is still at the bottom of that trunk. I left everything the way I'd found it when I closed up the store. But it makes me wonder . . . what was Mom's girdle doing there? Will there be a time when I need to use it for some emergency?

For now, though, I'll have to rely on my own charms to make people fall in love with me. Fortunately, I take after my mom. I'm pretty good at whipping up passionate frenzies. . . .

MAGICAL
LANDMARKS

SCENE: A room decorated with ornate tapestries, candles, and carpets in hues of purple, red, and gold. In the center is a golden throne on a dais. Apollo, dressed in jeans, a brilliant white T-shirt, a leather jacket, and sunglasses, lounges on the throne. On the wall is a neon sign that reads: FORTUNATELY APOLLO'S HERE!

APOLLO: Next!

[A girl camper enters]

GIRL: O, Great Apollo, god of prophecy, tell me, will I ever find love?

APOLLO: Find love? [mugs for the camera] I didn't know it was missing!

[Rim shot followed by canned laughter]

APOLLO: Next!

[A boy camper enters]

BOY: O, Great Apollo, god of prophecy, tell me, will I ever be rich?

APOLLO: What's your name, child?

BOY: Albert, Great Apollo.

APOLLO: Well, Albert Greatapollo, I foresee only one way for you to be rich. . . .

BOY: What is it?

APOLLO: [mugs for camera] Change your name to Richard.

[Rim shot followed by canned laughter]

APOLLO: Next!

[A different boy camper enters]

BOY #2: O, Great Apollo, god of prophecy, will I ever discover who my godly parent is?

APOLLO: Dear child, the answer is right in front of you.

BOY #2 [looking around]: Really? Where?

APOLLO: [stands up and spreads arms wide] Right in front of you.

BOY #2: I don't get it. Am I missing a clue?

APOLLO: You're missing a clue all right. [mugs for the camera] One might even call you *clueless*!

[Rim shot followed by canned laughter and prerecorded applause]

—From the comedy skit "Fortunately, Apollo's Here!" written by and starring Apollo

A comedy? Really? Man, I'm glad I didn't live through 1950s television. . . .
—P.J.

THE GROVE OF DODONA

*P*sst! Got wind chimes? Enjoy limericks? Want to know the future? Then hurry past Zephyros Creek and Zeus's Fist to the forest that holds this most ancient of all Oracles. Come on. It's not much farther. . . . Just follow the whispers. . . .

THE CAVE OF THE ORACLE

Brought to you by Pete the Palikos

Yo, demigods! Are you craving a great new hang-out? Word on the street is the Oracle's crib on Half-Blood Hill totally rocks. It's tricked out from top to bottom with purple curtains and massive sofas—with throw pillows for fresh pops of color, yo! Check out the graphic wall murals, graffiti quotes, and other funky artwork created by the one and only Delphic Oracle, Rachel Elizabeth Dare. You know what they say: if the torches are a-burnin', the prophecies are a-churnin'!

A CASE OF PPSS

by Rachel Elizabeth Dare

D o I scare you? I hope not. Most new campers think I'm über-spooky because I live part-time in a cave, have horrifying dreams about the end of the world, and spout enigmatic prophecies riddled with cheerful words such as *death*. Why anyone would find that disturbing is beyond me.

I delivered my first prophecy less than a minute after I accepted the spirit of Delphi. (If you want to know about the events triggered by *those* words, just ask any camper who lived through it. If you want to ask a camper who died through it, Nico di Angelo might set up a meet.) I thought I was prepared for the experience. I mean, I'd been channeling visions and seeing weird things most of my life. How different could mind-melding with an ancient spirit be?

Answer: very. Luckily, the god Apollo was on hand to help me to the Big House.

"You're experiencing PPSS," he said as he led me up the stairs and to an empty hospital bed.

"PPSS? What's that?" I asked right before I threw up into a nearby bin.

"Post-prophetic stress syndrome. Just lie still. It'll pass."

"You sure?"

He made a face. "Hello? God of prophecy, remember?"

"About that," I said. "Why do you need an Oracle? Why don't you dole out your own prophecies?"

He looked skyward and rendered his reply in haiku:

"I'm a free spirit
Adrift in sunshine and song.
Office hours bore me."

I thought about questioning whether *hours* was one syllable or two. But I let it slide, figuring he knew, seeing as he's the god of poetry.

Then I blurted out another question. "Why can't the Oracle have a boyfriend?"

I'm not sure why I asked. I wasn't interested in anyone. (Well, not anymore, anyway.) Guess I was just curious.

He didn't answer immediately. Instead, he broke off a leaf from a nearby laurel bough and crushed it between his finger and thumb. The air filled with its pungent aroma.

"Love can cloud the mind," he said at last. "An Oracle with an obstructed view is of no use." His voice was sorrowful, and I remembered that he had once been madly in love with a nymph named Daphne who turned into a laurel tree to escape his amorous attentions. I guess he knew about clouded minds.

I changed the subject. "Why do prophecies have to be so confusing? I mean, how come I can't just say straight up what's going to happen?"

He heaved a sigh, as if he'd answered the same question a million times before (which, given that he's immortal, maybe he had). "That would be as much fun as a two-piece jigsaw puzzle. Mystery, intrigue, hints of danger, unusual rhymes—those are what makes a memorable prophecy! Take this one, for instance:

> *"Pinochle and Ping-Pong, ambrosia squares and*
> *nectar,*
> *An attic with an Oracle, a disembodied leopard,*
> *A centaur in a wheelchair, a wine dude, serving time,*
> *This omphalus of Half-Blood will welcome offspring*
> *half-divine."*

Full disclosure: I had to look up *omphalus*. You hit the first syllable, by the way, like you would in

65

emphasis. The word means *navel*, as in the center point of something, not your belly button, though I suppose you could use it that way to impress your friends. *I might pierce my omphalus when I'm older.* Or mock your enemies. *You really don't know where your omphalus is? Ha-ha!*

But such navel contemplation came later. At that moment, Apollo was looking at me expectantly.

"Right," I said. "The prophecy describes Chiron, Dionysus, and the Big House, obviously."

"Obvious to you, sure," Apollo agreed. "But what if I told you that little prophetic nugget was delivered more than a thousand years ago?"

I had a sudden vision of people back then hearing the words *pinochle, Ping-Pong,* and *dude.* Gods only knew what they thought they meant. Food? Weapons? Clothing? They wouldn't have had a clue. And what did Chiron make of the bit about the centaur in a wheelchair?

The truth struck me like a cold, wet cloth to the face. Unless they were immortal, the people who heard that prophecy died without understanding what it meant. They may have gone crazy or even perished on quests attempting to decipher its meaning.

The thought made me really sad, then super-anxious about prophecies I might utter someday. "Apollo," I whispered, "will my words send people on hopeless quests?"

"Oh, Rachel." Apollo patted my hand comfortingly. "Yes."

"Well, that's just peachy." I didn't mean to sound bitter, but honestly, I was starting to have significant second thoughts about the whole Oracle gig.

Apollo stood up then. "You need sleep," he said. "But before I go, I have something for you." He pointed at the ceiling. A beam of golden light issued from his fingertip. A moment later, a present clumsily wrapped in gold foil paper thudded next to me. (I found out later that the beam of light almost gave the Stoll brothers heart attacks.) "Open it."

Inside was a rickety-looking three-legged stool. "Um . . . thanks?" I said.

"It's the original," he told me. "From Delphi. Well, from the Big House attic, more recently, where it languished underneath the posterior of your predecessor for far too long."

Understanding dawned on me. "This is *the* tripod of Delphi. The one the first Oracle sat on thousands of years ago. You're giving it to me?"

"I could have let you try stealing it, I suppose,"

Apollo said, scratching his head, "but that didn't go so well for Heracles when he tried it. He was punished with a year of women's work for his crime."

I cocked an eyebrow. "Excuse me? *Women's* work?"

Apollo waved dismissively. "Housework, chores, whatever. All that mattered was that for a blowhard like Heracles, washing dishes and sweeping floors was a well-deserved punch in the ego." He patted the stool lovingly. "The butts of many powerful women have rested here."

"I'm honored to be adding my derriere to the list." As the words came out of my mouth, I realized I meant it. For good or bad, I was the new Oracle of Delphi. I celebrated the momentous occasion by throwing up again.

Things have been a little quiet around my cave of late (unless you count my recent mural-eradicating, sofa-flipping, curtain-shredding tantrum, which I sincerely hope you won't). For some reason, the pilot light of prophecy has gone out, and Apollo hasn't been able to reignite it.

But don't worry. I predict I'll be spouting green smoke and confusion again by the time you're ready for a quest. And that will be soon, I have a feeling. . . .

THE MAGICAL BORDER

Brought to you by Pete the Palikos

Tired of living with mortals who smell of BO, cigars, and garlic? Then step through the border and leave the stench behind! Powered by the strongest Mist and guaranteed to repel even the most determined monsters* and nosiest mortals, this invisible barrier surrounds Camp Half-Blood with the best demigod protection magic can conjure. And that's not all! As an added bonus, inside the borders of camp, you'll be enveloped in delightful springtime weather all year round. So if you're ready to say good-bye to stink, slush, and certain death, come through the border today!

*Some restrictions apply. With invading armies and giant, hostile animated statues, results may vary.

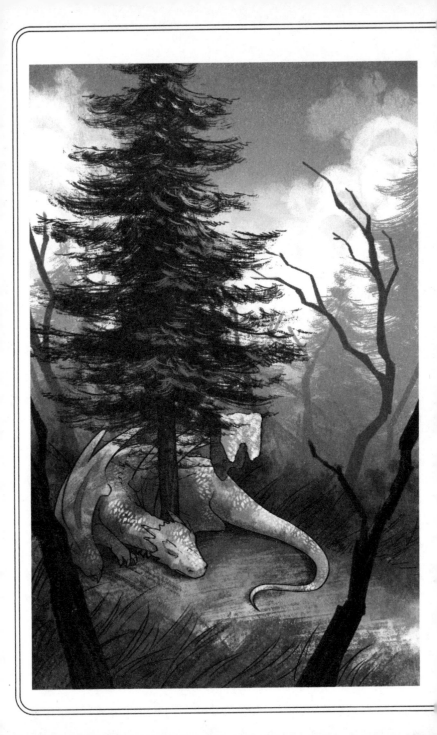

THALIA'S PINE AND THE GOLDEN FLEECE*

Brought to you by Pete the Palikos

Created by Zeus himself to embody the life essence of his dying daughter, Thalia Grace, this storied tree marks the easternmost boundary of Camp Half-Blood. The pine flourished for five years, strengthening the border with its magic. Then Luke Castellan, foul minion of Kronos, poisoned it with elder python venom. The valiant tree clung to life until the Golden Fleece, that ancient mystical blanket shorn from a flying ram, restored its vigor. The Fleece's curative powers even released Thalia from her piney imprisonment—*sap-free*! Today the Golden Fleece and the Athena Parthenos energize the camp's protective barriers, but the pine tree remains as a tribute to Thalia Grace's bravery. It also smells really nice.

> *Approach at your own risk. Peleus the guardian dragon only *appears* to be sleeping.

ON THE OUTSIDE
LOOKING IN

A CONVERSATION VIA VIDEOCONFERENCE WITH
SALLY JACKSON AND FREDERICK CHASE

by Thalia Grace and Leo Valdez

THALIA: Leo, did you get this stupid recording device working yet? What? I can't hear you! *What?* Gods, and people wonder why I joined Artem— Oh. Hi, everyone. Apparently, I'd muted Leo.

LEO: You'd be surprised how often people do that to me.

THALIA: Would I? So, we're talking with Sally Jackson, mother of Percy, and Frederick Chase, father of Annabeth, via a four-way videoconference setup that Leo *vows* will work just fine.

LEO: Did I vow? Not on the River Styx. I know better!

SALLY: Hello, Thalia, dear. You're looking particularly punk today. And Leo—

LEO: As smokin' hot as always, am I right?

SALLY: Well, smoking, anyway. You're smoldering through your T-shirt.

LEO: Whoops. Let me put me out. There.

THALIA: *Anyway* . . . we're here to get insight into

72

how mortal parents feel about Camp Half-Blood.
Ms. Jackson, Dr. Chase, you've never actually set
foot in the camp, is that right?

SALLY: That's correct. Even though I can see
through the Mist better than most mortals, I can't
get through the magic border. I suppose if someone
gave me direct permission to enter, I might be able
to, but even then, I'm not sure. The closest I ever got
was the summit of Half-Blood Hill, and honestly, I'm
not anxious to try that again.

LEO: Yeah, Peleus the dragon might snack on you.
Or the Athena Parthenos might zap you with her
laser-beam eyes. Wait . . . does the statue even have
laser-beam eyes, or is that just my wishful thinking?
Not that I'd want *you* to be zapped, Mrs. J.

SALLY: Thank you, dear, that's very comforting to
know.

THALIA: How about you, Dr. Chase?

FREDERICK [puts down model airplane he was
tinkering with]: Hmm? Oh, yes. Camp. No, never
been, though it would be fascinating to study from
a historical point of view. From what Annabeth
has told me, the only uninvited mortal to make it
through unscathed was Rachel Dare.

THALIA: I heard there was this pizza guy once . . . but

that's probably just a camp legend. Ms. Jackson, you may recall that I was there—in pine-tree mode—the first time Percy passed through. I don't remember it, though, because . . . well, I was a tree.

SALLY: I'm a little foggy on the details myself.

FREDERICK: Something about a Minotaur?

SALLY: *Everything* about a Minotaur.

THALIA: Can't say my first time at the border was much better. Fighting off monsters one minute, then—*ZAP!*—oozing tree sap the next.

FREDERICK: My word, Thalia, I just realized . . . I've never thanked you for saving Annabeth's life that day!

THALIA: It's ancient history, Dr. Chase, no worries.

FREDERICK: Perhaps I could ship you this model of Amelia Earhart's 1921 Kinner Airster biplane that I just finished. It's a lovely replica!

THALIA: That's really not necessary. But tell me, both of you, now that things have settled down in the demigod world, wouldn't you ever want to see Camp Half-Blood for yourselves?

SALLY: Well . . . yes, of course, if there were no Minotaurs or, ah, laser-beam-shooting impediments. In fact, after Percy's first summer there, I *did* ask Chiron if he'd open the camp for just one day so families could visit. Mortal families, that is.

LEO: I'm guessing Chiron said no.

SALLY: Yes.

LEO: Wait . . . he said yes?

SALLY: No, he said no.

LEO: I'm confused.

THALIA: What else is new?

SALLY: Chiron told me that he did have a visitors' day once, about a hundred years ago. But it did not go well.

THALIA: What happened?

SALLY: Somehow an eidolon, a manticore, and a disgruntled Party Pony found out about it. The eidolon possessed a camper's half sister, the centaur got his hands on a cap of invisibility, and the manticore disguised himself as a family dog. They infiltrated the camp.

THALIA: Not a bad plan, though I prefer a direct assault myself.

SALLY: It might have worked, except the centaur wasn't the sharpest *kopis* in the drawer. He couldn't help showing off during the archery exhibition. Shot three bull's-eyes before someone noticed the bow was floating in midair.

THALIA: What about the manticore and the eidolon?

SALLY: They caught the manticore spiking the

volleyballs. With its tail spikes, that is, not actually hitting the balls over the net.

THALIA: Volleyball existed a hundred years ago?

FREDERICK: Yes, indeed! Volleyball, or *mintonette* as it was originally called, was invented in 1895 by William G. Morgan in— Sorry. Once a professor, always a professor.

SALLY: The eidolon caused the most destruction. It hurled a jar of Greek fire at the climbing wall, which then dripped with flames for hours afterward. That's where Chiron came up with the idea of adding lava as a permanent feature for the wall, by the way.

THALIA: That Chiron. Always finding ways to turn death-defying challenges into much worse death-defying challenges. So what happened to the intruders?

LEO: Festus!

FREDERICK: Gesundheit.

SALLY: I think he means Festus, his bronze dragon.

LEO: The one and only! You know he was originally built for border patrol, right? What I heard, he had a killer body back then. Like, literally—he had this spiky exterior plating so he could use his body to kill. Man, I bet he body-slammed that manticore right back to Tartarus!

SALLY: Chiron did mention there had been some body-slamming. As for the eidolon, it took the combined powers of Aphrodite's children to charmspeak the spirit out of the girl.

LEO: And the centaur?

SALLY: Chiron sorted out the cause of his fellow centaur's anger—something about not getting his fair share of root beer the last time he was at camp. Chiron, being kindhearted, let him return to his tribe with a warning. But the camp hasn't held another visitors' day since.

THALIA: I guess I see why. And now that I think about it, a family day might be depressing for some of the campers who don't *have* family. I mean . . . who'd come visit me? Or Leo?

LEO: Speak for yourself, Tree Girl. I may not have much family, but all the ladies would flock to me like moths to my flame. Aw, yeah!

THALIA: Aw, *yech.*

FREDERICK: Now, now. We'd visit both of you! Er, that is, if you *do* schedule a visitors' day, and if I can remember to put the date on my calendar. . . .

SALLY: [coughs] I think the important thing is that I know Percy and the rest of you have a safe place to be. I don't feel a driving need to see the camp for myself. It's just comforting to know that when my son is there, he's with friends who have his back.

LEO: Also his front, his sides, and his top. I draw the line at his bottom, though.

SALLY: However, there is something I'd like to get on the record. Something I think all mortal parents would agree with.

THALIA: Sure, go ahead, Ms. Jackson.

SALLY: Demigods, we love you.

FREDERICK: Agreed.

SALLY: But if you don't start Iris-messaging us a little more often, we're going to sic Coach Hedge on you. Take care of yourselves, and make us proud. You always do!

THE ATHENA PARTHENOS

Brought to you by Pete the Palikos

Recently recovered from a massive spiderweb deep within the bowels of Rome, this priceless forty-foot-tall chryselephantine* statue of the goddess Athena is accessorized with a sphinx-and-griffin crown, a handheld statue of the goddess Nike, a shield, and a snake. It exudes its protective and somewhat fierce magic from its new home atop Half-Blood Hill.

*chryselephantine: sculpted of gold and ivory

A PEPLOS FOR ATHENA

by Malcolm Pace

Ask anyone here and they'll tell you I'm a level-headed guy. Big on logic, small on drama. A think-first, leap-second sort of demigod. Comes with being Athena's kid, I guess.

So I was a little freaked-out when the visions started hitting me.

Demigods have nightmares regularly—as you'll find out soon enough, I'm afraid. But these visions would happen when I was awake. I'd be walking along, not a care in the world, when—*BAM*! My brain would be flooded with images of some ancient Greek festival. I saw athletic events like in the Olympics, plus musical contests, poetry readings, and even beauty pageants. I witnessed winners receiving amphorae of olive oil (super valuable back then). I watched a parade that ended with a life-size wooden statue of Athena being ceremoniously draped with a huge colorful cloth.

This mental slide show scrolled through my mind on four separate occasions. By the fourth rerun, I wanted answers. One, what the heck was this festival?

Two, where were the visions coming from? And three, why was I having them?

I got the answer to the first question by doing a little digging in our cabin's research library. Buried in one book was a description of a festival called the Great Panathenaia that was held every four years in Athens in honor of my mother. I learned that the wooden statue was the Athena Polias, meaning Athena "of the city," and the cloth was a special peplos (a versatile garment that could be worn as a floor-length skirt, a top-and-skirt ensemble, a shawl, or— Gods, I sound like Valentina! Sorry!) woven with images depicting Athena's greatest triumphs, like the time she defeated the giant Enceladus.

So I'd been seeing the Great Panathenaia. Now I just had to figure out where the visions were coming from and why I was seeing them.

The "where" proved surprisingly easy to solve. Every time the visions hit me, I was near Half-Blood Hill. Therefore, my logical brain told me, something in that area was causing the visions. Conclusion: the something was the Athena Parthenos.

If you don't believe that's possible, just go up to Half-Blood Hill and experience the Athena Parthenos's power for yourself. The statue radiates magic. Its eyes follow you. It's so lifelike, you expect it to speak. Trust me, once you feel its power, you'll understand why I decided the statue was channeling the pictures from the past into my head.

So that left the question of why. I explored several possibilities but kept coming back to one: Mom was giving me a not-so-subtle hint. I deduced she missed having a festival dedicated just to her. I further deduced she wanted me to resurrect that festival here at Camp Half-Blood. She would never come right out and tell me that, of course. Demanding to be honored isn't her style. That's why she used the statue as a go-between.

Just to be sure I was right, though, I whispered my conclusions to the Athena Parthenos. Yes, I felt a little silly talking to a statue, and of course, the statue didn't reply. Neither did Mom. Not directly, anyway. But that night, an amphora of olive oil appeared beside my bunk. This either meant she was giving me a favorable omen or she wanted me to make a *whole lot* of pizza. I figured it was the former.

The next morning, I told my siblings and Chiron everything. The Athena kids were all over remaking the festival. Chiron himself had attended the original

Panathenaia back in the day, so he readily greenlit the project.

Our inaugural Camp Half-Blood Panathenaia is scheduled for next August, to coincide with the dates of the original festival and Mom's "sprang from Zeus's head" day. That gives us Athena kids about a year to construct a wooden Athena Polias statue, weave a ginormous peplos, organize the competitions, and plan the procession. (Some of my siblings suggested just making a peplos for the Athena Parthenos, but firstly I don't think there's enough cloth on Long Island to make a serape that big, and secondly the ancient Athenians didn't do it that way. They used a wooden statue made especially for the festival. I want to do it the traditional way because, well, this is all about bringing back a tradition.)

Am I worried we'll be ready in time? Nah. As children of Athena, planning and organizing runs in our blood. Plus, other campers are already volunteering to help. If you want to lend a hand, the sign-up sheet is on Cabin Six's door.

And Mom? I think she approves. The last time I was near the Athena Parthenos, I swear it winked.

TRAINING
GROUNDS

SCENE: Apollo jogs backward along the beachfront, shooting arrows from his golden bow. He's followed by campers dressed in combat gear, jogging in military formation.

APOLLO: I don't know but I've been told!

CAMPERS: We don't know but we've been told!

APOLLO: The sun god's got a bow of gold!

CAMPERS: The sun god's got a bow of gold!

APOLLO: He's the best shot in the land!

CAMPERS: He's the best shot in the land!

APOLLO: Augh! [Apollo trips and lands on his backside] I've fallen in the sand!

CAMPERS [jogging circles around him]: Augh! He's fallen in the sand!

APOLLO: I meant to do that, so don't laugh!

CAMPERS: He meant to do that, so don't laugh!

APOLLO [tries to get up but falls back again]: Ow! I hurt my godly calf!

CAMPERS: Ow! He hurt his godly calf!

APOLLO [glowering and starting to glow]: If you want to live another day . . .

CAMPERS: If we want to live another day . . .

APOLLO [radiating brighter]: STOP REPEATING WHAT I SAY!

CAMPERS: STOP—um . . .

—Military cadence written, chanted, and abruptly ended by Apollo

Best. Scene. Ever.
–P.J.

THE ARMORY

Centrally located and stocked to the rafters with spears, swords, daggers, shields, bows and arrows, and clubs, the armory is a must-see for those in need of deadly weapons. Dig through, and you might even find one imbued with magical abilities. So don't delay—your stabber, slicer, slasher, or basher awaits!

THE CLIMBING WALL

Brought to you by Pete the Palikos

Where is fun spelled *l-a-v-a*? The climbing wall, of course! Originally created to fine-tune reflexes and test hand-eye coordination, the climbing wall has become every camper's top spot for primal-screaming practice. If a fall from halfway up the side doesn't send you to the Big House infirmary, the slamming walls or molten magma will. So come on up—just don't look down!

THE COMBAT ARENA AND THE ARCHERY RANGE

Brought to you by Pete the Palikos

More demigod blood has been shed in this circular fighting zone than anywhere else in camp. So what are you waiting for? Strap on your armor and get ready to sweat, because you ain't *never* had a workout like this before! You'll engage every muscle as you slash with your sword, jab with your spear, smash with your shield, and stab with your dagger. And that's just the warm-up! Now that your blood is pumping (inside your body, outside your body, whatever), it's time to test your metal against a straw dummy—or to test your *mettle* against a live opponent. But remember: the hits are real and so is the blood, so keep your guard up!

Striking from afar more your style? We've got you covered! Just a javelin's throw from the combat arena is the archery range, with its array of boldly colored targets, their bull's-eyes daring you to hit them with a well-aimed arrow. Just be on the lookout for errant projectiles so you don't become a target yourself!

THE ARES PEACETIME CHALLENGE

by Ellis Wakefield

To be a great head counselor, you have to be more than just the oldest sibling in a cabin. You have to be a leader—smart, strong, decisive, brave—and also a fearless fighter. Clarisse La Rue, our previous head counselor, was all those things and more. Sherman Yang? Him, I wasn't so sure about.

Sherman took over when Clarisse left Camp Half-Blood to go to college. He was a typical Ares kid, meaning a ferocious muscle-bound fighting machine with a yen for bloody conflict and a disdain for peace. But as impressive as those qualities were, I wondered if they were enough to lead our cabin. More importantly, were they enough to lead us to victory over the other cabins? If not . . . well, let's just say I was secretly studying him to find his Achilles' heel.

Not long after Sherman took over, Ares cabin scored poorly on the daily camp inspection. One of my sisters had left a plate of sticky, sweet barbecue under her bunk, and ants had swarmed it. Not the gigantic *myrmekes*—they prefer shiny things to smoked meats. It would have been okay if the myrmekes had invaded, actually. Things had been so calm lately, I wouldn't have minded going a few rounds with them, sword versus mandible.

Anyway, our chore that day was combat arena and archery range prep. I loved practicing in the fighting zones, but tidying up afterward and getting everything ready for the next session? I'd rather tackle the Nemean Lion, and from the looks on my cabinmates' faces, they felt the same way. We might have staged a sit-down if nonaggressive protest didn't sicken us so much.

Instead, we trudged out to the arenas. To my surprise, a number of campers from other cabins were there too. So was Sherman, which kind of surprised me, because he normally wasn't the first one on-site when we had to do chores.

"Ares cabin!" he barked. "Take a knee!"

I didn't get what was going on. We were supposed to be doing prep. And why were all these other campers here? Nevertheless, we Ares kids knelt as one and waited to see what would happen.

"I'm running a friendly little relay race today,"

Sherman announced to the whole crowd. "Who wants in?"

The Ares kids all started raising our hands, naturally. I still didn't understand why Sherman was holding a race instead of making us do our assigned tasks, but I wasn't going to argue.

He gestured at us impatiently. "No, no, not you, Ares cabin. You're just here as observers. This race is in the arena and archery range, and you know those areas too well. It wouldn't be fair to the other competitors."

Fair? How could *this* guy be the head of our cabin? I almost stormed away in disgust. But then I noticed the crafty twinkle in Sherman's eye. He was up to something. What, I didn't know. But I wanted to find out.

"What do we win?" asked Cecil Markowitz. That kid, always thinking about the potential payout.

Sherman smiled slyly. "Whoever finishes first gets to fire the T-shirt gun tonight."

His announcement caused a ripple of excitement. Guns weren't a big favorite at Camp Half-Blood; most campers preferred the traditional weapons of ancient Greece. The Ares cabin T-shirt gun was one of the few exceptions. It shot tightly rolled Half-Blood tees fifty feet in the air. It was a real crowd-pleaser during camp sing-alongs and volleyball matches.

After some jostling and debate, five contestants stood up to volunteer: Will Solace, Miranda Gardiner, Billie Ng, Cecil Markowitz, and Damien White. My money was on Will or Damien to win whatever Sherman had cooked up. Will, because he was clever and quick. Damien, because he was devious.

"Competitors!" Sherman held up a hand, fingers splayed. "This race consists of five tasks, which are as follows: Each of you must sharpen the blades of two practice swords. Then you must replace four used archery targets with new ones. After that, you polish a shield. Then you must replace the points on three spears. Finally, reattach a straw dummy's limbs and head. Then return here to me." Sherman curled his fingers into a fist. "Any questions?"

I was biting the inside of my cheek to keep the smirk off my face. I had to give it to Sherman—he'd come up with a great plan to get the other campers to do our work. Nothing like the promise of firing a large gun to keep people from thinking straight.

Sherman lined up the racers and bellowed, "Go!"

Off they raced. Twenty minutes later, Miranda crossed the finish line first. Gasping, she raised a triumphant fist in the air. Sherman grabbed her in a hug, then quickly let go, red-faced and grinning sheepishly. We Ares kids cheered lustily for the victor, for the chores we didn't have to do, and most of all, for Sherman—our ace head counselor.

THE VOLLEYBALL COURT

Brought to you by Pete the Palikos

Whether you're a serious player or just a camper looking for a little fun competish, there's no better place than the volleyball court to feel the sun on your back, the wind in your hair, or a ball in your face. Come to play, come to watch, come to catch a T-shirt from the Ares cabin's gun—just come!

GAME CHANGER

by Laurel and Holly Victor

LAUREL: Check it—we're in charge of the volleyball court.

HOLLY: We keep it ready to go.

LAUREL: Makes me sick.

HOLLY: The court?

LAUREL: No, that campers play for fun, as in—

HOLLY: Don't say it!

LAUREL: —*recreationally.*

HOLLY: Gross! Pointless!

LAUREL: Totally goes against our heritage.

HOLLY: True that. Ancient Greeks loved organized competitive sports.

LAUREL: Hello, ever hear of the Olympics?

HOLLY: Or the Panathenaia?

LAUREL: Sand courts were everywhere back then. Ancient Greeks wrestled and boxed in them.

HOLLY: Called them *palaestrae.* Singular: *palaestra.*

LAUREL: After Palaestra, the goddess who invented wrestling.

HOLLY: Hear that, boys? The *goddess* of wrestling.

LAUREL: Girl power!

HOLLY: They wrestled naked.

LAUREL: So no place to hide weapons.

HOLLY: Palaestra ruled the ring.

LAUREL: Like we rule the court.

HOLLY: Victors 20, Opponents 0. Can I get an *Oh, yeah!*?

LAUREL: Oh, yeah! Know who I'd like to take on?

HOLLY: I know who *I'd* like to take on.

LAUREL and HOLLY: The Hunters.

HOLLY: Check it, newbies. When the Hunters are at camp, we play capture the flag.

LAUREL: Hunters 56, Half-Blood 0. Unacceptable result.

HOLLY: So I'm hiding the flags the next time they show.

LAUREL: Can't play capture the flag without flags to capture!

HOLLY: Then we'll throw down a volleyball challenge.

LAUREL: Victors versus Hunters. Two of them against the two of us.

HOLLY: Those Hunters? They'll look like frightened prey.

LAUREL: Deer looking down the wrong end of an arrow.

HOLLY: Mixed-green salad looking down the wrong end of a fork.

LAUREL: What?

HOLLY: I'm going vegetarian.

LAUREL: Hey, me too.

HOLLY: Since when?

LAUREL: Since before you decided to.

HOLLY: I decided it first!

LAUREL: Did not.

HOLLY: Did too.

LAUREL: This conversation is over.

HOLLY: It's over when I say it's over!

LAUREL and HOLLY: It's over!

TINKERING

THE FORGE

So you're taking a walk in the wild, minding your own business, when—*WHAM!*—a chunk of Celestial bronze falls from the sky and almost kills you. What do you do now? I'll tell you what: you bring that bronze on down to the hottest place in camp—the forge! Cabin Nine campers will jump at the chance to hammer the mystical metal into a weapon, a shield, armor, or even—wink, wink—a helmet! While there, you might catch a glimpse of everyone's favorite Cyclops, Tyson. And maybe you can get the Hephaestus kids to ask their dad to watch where he tosses his scraps next time.

THE ARTS AND CRAFTS CENTER

Brought to you by Pete the Palikos

Creative juices flow freely in this airy studio. It's a favorite place of Athena's children, who come to sculpt, paint, weave, and do ceramics, but anyone is welcome to embrace their artistic side here (also their artistic front and top, but please refrain from embracing bottoms). Skeins of naturally dyed yarn, easels with stretched canvases, blocks of marble and clay, and all the tools and paints you could ask for await!

BUNKER NINE

This cavernous workshop lies underground, nestled deep in the woods at the foot of the western hills. Bunker Nine was sealed following the first demigod civil war and eventually lost to memory. For more than one hundred and fifty years, it sat like a time capsule waiting to be discovered. But now, thanks to the fiery touch of Leo Valdez, its secrets and mechanical supplies are within reach. Are you curious enough to venture in?

NUMBER 130
IN BUNKER NINE

by Nyssa Barrera

Bunker Nine is an amazing place. But if you're ever there, steer clear of the shadowy corner way in back. Something bad sits there. If you do decide to look, take my advice: don't touch it. Think I'm kidding? Read on.

Late one afternoon, Connor Stoll, Sherman Yang, Valentina Diaz, Paolo Montes, Butch Walker, and I were hanging out on the beach when talk turned to camp curses.

"Remember the rhyming-couplet curse Apollo cabin threw that time?" Butch asked. " 'I'm coming in your direction / So get ready for cabin inspection!' "

Valentina giggled. "My cabin did one years ago called the sweetie curse. Anyone with a secret crush was compelled to call the object of their affection 'sweetie.' " She glanced at Paolo from under her lashes. "I wonder what would happen if I hurled that curse now?"

Paolo beamed uncomprehendingly.

Sherman nudged my shoulder. "What about you, Nyssa? Got any good curse stories?"

I shifted uncomfortably. "Just one."

"Well? Let's hear it."

"I can't. It's more something I would have to *show.*"

I wanted to drop the subject, but they wouldn't let it go. They just kept cajoling me until finally I said, "All right. Fine. Wait here."

I ran back to my cabin and retrieved an old book from my storage locker. The book's coal-black leather cover had orange lettering stamped into it, and a small keyhole padlock kept it closed. Reluctantly, I brought it back to the beach. Valentina squealed when she saw it.

"That's a vintage diary, isn't it?" she asked. "They sold them in the camp store back in the fifties!"

"This one is from the forties," I corrected. "It belonged to Heloise, one of my siblings. I found it stashed behind a false panel under my bunk."

Valentina rubbed her hands eagerly. "OMG, I *love* reading other people's diaries! Uh, not that I would ever do that without permission, of course," she added hurriedly.

"So what does Heloise's diary have to do with curses?" Sherman asked.

"Everything," I said grimly. "Listen."

June 10, 1948

Diary:

Back at camp. This summer's project: a race car that runs on Greek fire.

June 13, 1948

Diary:

Sketches complete. Materials gathered. Construction starts tomorrow.

June 16, 1948

Diary:

Outraged. Caught a son of Aphrodite poking around my stuff. Claims he's a car fanatic and came to check out my wheels. Lies, most likely.

June 17, 1948

Diary:

The boy came back. He asked questions about my car. Smart questions. Might have misjudged him.

June 19, 1948

    Dear Diary:

    James has blond hair and sky-blue eyes. Girls are in love with him. The naiads, too. They dragged him into the lake today and almost drowned him. Ridiculous.

June 20, 1948

    Dear Diary:

    James brought me a jar of Greek fire at lunch today. All the other girls stared at me.

June 22, 1948

    Dear Diary:

    The car is finished. I put in butter-yellow leather seats and painted it sky blue.

June 26, 1948

    Dear Diary:

    First test-drive successful! James wanted to do it, but I wouldn't let him. If anything bad happened, I'd want it to happen to me. . . .

June 28, 1948

    Dearest Diary:

    James says he wants to be an actor someday, but if that

doesn't work out, maybe he'll be a race-car driver—but only if I design his car. I think he was joking.

June 30, 1948
    Dearest Diary:
    The second test-drive was even better. I let James put in the Greek fire. A little must have leaked out because when our hands touched, my fingers burned.

July 2, 1948
    Dearest Diary:
    James drove the car around the chariot track today. The other girls watched him. He hugged me after and said the car's engine purrs like a kitten.

July 2, 1948 (midnight)
    Dearest Diary:
    I'm purring too.

July 3, 1948
    Dearest Diary:
    Tomorrow night there will be fireworks on the beach. I'll help set them up. Then I'll look for James.

July 4, 1948

    Diary:

    I found him. With an Ares girl.

July 5, 1948

    Diary:

    The car exploded in the middle of the night. I told Chiron it was the Greek fire. I told James I'm not building another one.

July 8, 1948

    Diary:

    James visits the armory a lot these days.

July 10, 1948:

    Diary:

    I have a new project: Harmonia's necklace.

The diary ended there.

I took a deep breath and looked at my friends. They were staring at me with rapt attention.

"Harmonia was the daughter of Ares and Aphrodite," I told them. "As you probably know, Aphrodite was my dad's wife. When Hephaestus found out about Harmonia . . . well, he wasn't too happy with Aphrodite. He fashioned a cursed item."

Valentina put her hand to her mouth. "He *cursed* my mom?"

"Not her—Harmonia. He made a beautiful cursed necklace and gave it to her on her wedding day. The rest of her life was basically misery. Same for anyone who wore the necklace after her."

Butch frowned. "So what does Harmonia's story have to do with Heloise and James?"

Valentina rolled her eyes. "You're so thick! Heloise, daughter of Hephaestus, was in love with James, son of Aphrodite. Then she caught him with a daughter of Ares. The love triangle repeated."

I nodded. "And then Heloise started working on a project called Harmonia's necklace."

"A curse for the boyfriend who jilted her," Sherman said.

"Yeah." I showed them a black-and-white photograph of a cute teenage boy in an old-fashioned Camp Half-Blood T-shirt, sitting next to a girl who looked like a younger version of Rosie the Riveter. "James and Heloise in 1948. And this is James in 1955."

I pulled out a close-up of a twentysomething man

with chiseled features and a sultry expression. "Anyone recognize him?"

Valentina's jaw dropped. "It's James Dean!"

"The sausage tycoon?" Butch asked.

"Not *Jimmy* Dean, you idiot. *James* Dean. The actor." Valentina smoothed her hand over the photo. "He was a total hottie."

"Hottie!" Paolo confirmed in a heavy Brazilian accent. "*Rebel. Eden.* Dead young."

"Right," I said. "James Dean rocketed to superstardom in 1955 with two movies, *East of Eden* and *Rebel Without a Cause.*"

"What did Paolo mean by 'dead young'?" Connor asked.

I showed them a third photo of James. He was sitting in a sleek silver race car with the number 130 painted on the hood and sides. "This was taken around September twenty-second, 1955. Nice car, huh? It's a Porsche 550 Spyder." I laid down one last photo. "And *this* was taken on September thirtieth."

They all gasped. The Spyder was a mangled wreck of twisted metal, identifiable only by the number 130.

"James and a friend were driving to Salinas, California, for a race," I told them. "They stopped at a roadside store. The accident happened about half an hour later. James was killed in the crash." I chewed my lip. "I think Heloise cursed the car when it was at the rest stop. She installed something, enchanted the chassis. I don't know, exactly, but that was her secret project, code-named Harmonia's necklace."

Sherman frowned. "Car accidents happen all the time, Nyssa."

"Yeah, but listen to this: the guy who hit them claims he never saw the car coming. After the crash, parts salvaged from the Spyder were installed in other cars—and *those* cars were in horrible accidents. The wreck itself toppled from a truck bed and crushed a man's leg. A pair of thieves suffered freak injuries while trying to steal the steering wheel and seat covers. A garage housing the Spyder's remains caught fire—but the car itself was untouched. Need I go on?"

"Where's the car now?" Sherman asked.

"It vanished in 1959. No mortal knows where it is."

"Hang on," Butch said. *"No mortal?"*

I gazed toward the western hills. "It's in Bunker Nine. I think my dad hid it there. Or maybe Heloise did, to prevent the curse from hurting any more people." I looked at them. "Or to keep it as a trophy of her success."

So that's the story. Maybe the curse on number 130 has faded. You want to touch that wreck in the shadows and find out, be my guest. Me, I'm steering clear.

WILD PLACES

SCENE: The set of a game show. Three campers sit behind a table with dinger bells in front of them. Apollo stands behind a podium. He's dressed as a cheesy game show host—open shirt, bright gold lamé jacket, skinny black pants.

APOLLO: Welcome to our first annual Camp Half-Blood quiz show! Please give a warm welcome to our contestants. From Athena cabin . . . Bea Wise! [applause] From Ares cabin . . . Arnold Beefcake! [applause] And representing our cloven-hoofed friends . . . Ferdinand Underwood the satyr! [hoof stomps] Contestants, you know the rules. I ask a question. If you know the answer, ding your bell. Are you ready?

WISE [tapping temple]: I think, therefore I am.

BEEFCAKE [flexing]: Do your worst!

UNDERWOOD: Um, I ate my bell.

APOLLO: Excellent! Then let's begin. First question: Name the serpent I slayed.

[Ding-ding!]

APOLLO: Wise?

WISE: That's not a question.

APOLLO: Sorry, "That's not a question" is incorrect.

WISE: No, wait, I meant—

[Ding-ding!]

BEEFCAKE: The serpent was Python!

APOLLO: Correct!

BEEFCAKE [showing two thumbs-up]: Ayyyyy!

APOLLO: Next question—

UNDERWOOD: So, should I just say *ding-ding* if I know the answer or—?

APOLLO: Who falsely accused me of flaying him alive after a music contest?

UNDERWOOD: Blaa-blaa!

APOLLO: I'm sorry, "blaa-blaa!" is incorrect. Also, you didn't ring in. The correct answer is Marsyas the satyr.

WISE: Hang on! I knew that! You didn't give me a chance to answer!

APOLLO: He thought he was so great on those stupid twin pipes, but I showed him.

BEEFCAKE: Yeah, you did!

WISE: I thought you were *falsely* accused.

UNDERWOOD: Blaa-blaa!

APOLLO: Final question: Do you know what time it is?

[Ding-ding!]

WISE [checks sun's location]: Two twen—

APOLLO: It's dancing time! [rips off jacket and shirt and starts Hula-Hooping] Hit it, boys!

[Satyrs enter flailing ribbon sticks and tootling on reed pipes, and cavort about the sun god]

BEEFCAKE: Oh, yeah! [rips off shirt, twirls it in the air] Now it's a party!

WISE [rubbing temples]: I can't believe I studied for this.

FERDINAND: Ding-ding?

Ahhh! My retinas!
–P.J.

GROVE OF THE COUNCIL OF CLOVEN ELDERS

Brought to you by Pete the Palikos

Scouting around for a place of natural beauty for your next meeting? Consider reserving this idyllic, out-of-the-way clearing! Majestic old-growth trees surround a blanket of soft grass. Leaves rustle in the gentle breezes wafting in from the nearby shore. It's a short hike north of the pegasus stables but worth every step. Iris-message ahead and the forest dryads will arrange for snacks and drinks.

> Note: Special permission needed to use the rosebush topiary thrones.

LIVE AND LEARN . . . SO YOU CAN KEEP LIVING

by Woodrow the Satyr

I was honored when Percy Jackson asked me to tell you about the survival-skills class I teach. Honored but puzzled, because I teach Reed Pipe Music Composition and Appreciation, not Survival 101.

So I sent paper-airplane letters to two satyrs who'd taught the class before, Grover Underwood and Gleeson Hedge, to ask for their advice. Here are their replies:

[Sent on a slightly chewed brown paper bag]

Dear Woodrow,

California is dry. Thanks for asking.

I used the KISS approach—Keep It Simple, Satyr—when I taught the class, because so many students were ADHD. Here, in a nutshell, is my lesson plan. (If you don't have a nutcracker, you can probably borrow one from the dining pavilion dryads.)

Step one: Scan your surroundings for immediate threats. Examples: Fast-approaching monsters with claws deployed and fangs dripping venom; cavernous pits rimmed with rotten banana peels; clowns (both happy- and sad-faced).

Step two: Take inventory. Helpful items to look for: Water. Food. Fire. More food.

Step three: Stay put and wait for rescue. Note: This last step only works if others are looking for you.

Hope this helps!

Wildly yours,

Grover

[Written on the back of a crayon drawing of a daddy satyr, a mommy wind nymph, and a tiny baby kid]

Woodrow,

Surviving is all about beating the odds. Also the evens. Those evens can be sneaky, so *don't take your eyes off them!*

As for the beating, you can't go wrong with a sturdy length of wood. Ash is best—strong, lightweight, makes an excellent *crack* sound when it connects with its target. Stay away from pine. Smells nice, but too sticky. And you never know who might be living inside it.

If you don't have a club handy, try a hoof-kick

to the solar plexus, a horn-stab to the throat, and a rump-butt to the gut. Boo-ya!

Coach

I appreciated this sage advice but decided to seek my own technique for survival training. So I did what I often do when contemplating a challenge: I looked to the stars for guidance. That's when it hit me—I could teach demigods to look to the stars for guidance!

Constellations are awesome orientation and navigation tools. They have great historic significance, too, since they're made up of beings and people placed in the heavens by the Greek gods. So it was a win-win concept.

Here's a little taste of my proposed lesson plan:

Whatever, Mother (Or the W-M-Shaped Constellation)

Cassiopeia, queen of Ethiopia, bragged that she and her daughter, Andromeda, were more beautiful than Poseidon's girls, the Nereids.

"Gods, Mother, embarrass me much?" groaned Andromeda.

The Nereids complained to their dad. As punishment for Cassiopeia's boast, Poseidon sent Cetus the sea monster to wreak havoc on Ethiopia. The only way to end the reign of terror was to sacrifice Andromeda to the beast.

Naturally, Cassiopeia didn't tell her daughter that. Instead, she lured Andromeda to the coast with promises of a lovely spa day by the sea. Once there, she chained her to a rock within easy snacking distance of Cetus.

"Mo-*ther*!" Andromeda was heard to complain over the pounding of the waves. "These chains clash with my outfit! The salt spray is making my hair frizz! And when is my masseuse getting here?"

"Here he comes now!" Cassiopeia called back as Cetus reared out of the surf and charged the princess. (Note: Grover would have identified Cetus as an "immediate threat.")

Seconds before the monster struck, a figure swooped out of the sky. It was the hero Perseus! He drew his sword of diamonds ("Ooo! Shiny!" Andromeda was heard to say over Cetus's snarls), slew the beast, freed Andromeda, controlled her frizz with smoothing serum, and married her. They had nine children, founded the city of Mycenae, and lived happily ever after.

When they died, Perseus and Andromeda were turned into constellations. They're so dim, though, that they can be hard to find. Instead, look for Cassiopeia, who was also set in the stars. As pushy in the heavens as she was on Earth, you can't miss her pattern: five bright stars that form a *W* or *M* shape, depending on how you look at it. Find it, and you're on the right track to getting home.

FYI: Mother and daughter constellations are very close to each other. So close, in fact, that if you listen in on a moonless night, you can hear Andromeda telling Cassiopeia to "back off and give her some space already."

BEAR WITH ME

Zeus was sneaking around behind Hera's back—again—with a lovely female named Callisto, who happened to be one of Artemis's Hunters. Why Callisto broke her vow to stay away from men is anyone's guess. Some say Zeus tricked her by disguising himself as Artemis.

Hera found out about Zeus's infidelity—again—and with one angry *poof* turned Callisto into a bear, which she then asked Artemis to hunt. Or maybe she asked Arcas, who was Zeus and Callisto's son and a skilled archer. The details are a little murky. Either way, Callisto the bear was staring down the pointy end of a drawn arrow when Zeus finally took notice.

"Hmm. This may be partially my fault," Zeus confessed as he defused the threat. Callisto reared up on her hind legs, crossed her paws over her hairy chest, and gave him the bear version of "You *think?*"

"Let me make it up to you." He transformed her into stars and lobbed them into the sky. He did the same for Arcas, figuring the boy would be safe from Hera that way. The stars formed patterns that looked like bears, which is why the Greeks named them the Big Dipper and the Little Dipper.

Ha-ha! Just kidding! The Greeks called them Ursa Major and Ursa Minor, or the Great Bear and the Little Bear. Ursa Major looks like a—well, like a big water dipper, actually, with a bent handle and a wide-mouthed bowl. Ursa Minor is a smaller version of a dipper with a handle that bends up instead of down.

FYI: Rumor has it that Zeus and Callisto secretly hang out when he's in his Roman form. He hides in the planet Jupiter—or maybe he becomes the planet Jupiter—and she revolves around him in the nearby moon named after her. Watch for a supernova in that quadrant of the sky when Hera discovers their trysts.

LOOK TO THE STARS FOR GUIDANCE

So, how do these stories help if you're lost? If you can pick out Ursa Major, Ursa Minor, and Cassiopeia in the night sky, you can find north. The three constellations are bunched up around Polaris, the one fixed star in the sky. Find the constellations, and you can find Polaris. Find Polaris, and you've found north. Find north, and you can figure out where east, west, and south are. And then you're as good as home!

Note: When I shared my lesson plan with Grover, he pointed out that this method of navigation only works if you know in which direction your home lies. Also, it has proven to be less effective during daylight hours. Oh, well. It's a start.

THE PEGASUS STABLES

Brought to you by Pete the Palikos

Winged horses need a place to call home, too, and Camp Half-Blood is delighted that some have made theirs here. Cleaning the stables might not be much fun, but the flights more than make up for it. So if you fancy a horse-powered swoop through the sky, stop by and meet the herd—and be sure to bring donuts!

THE MYRMEKES' LAIR

Brought to you by Pete the Palikos

This site should come with a warning sign: KEEP OUT! If ever you find yourself near the monstrous anthill, be sure to ditch any shiny metal you might have on your person. The giant ants find it irresistible. What they *don't* like are certain waterways. The Zephyros Creek runs between the main campgrounds and the ants' lair, which is probably why they haven't invaded—though the queen ant might just do a flyby sometime. If they ever decide to cross Long Island Sound, however, New York City could be in for a world of hurt.

THE GEYSERS

Come to a land apart . . . a land of misty magic and moist tropical breezes, where delightful humidity thickens the air and kisses your skin until it glows. You'll know you're near when sweat trickles down your back, dampens your hair, and weighs down your clothes. Once here, give voice to your offering to the geyser gods—a poem, a song, or a joke told with spot-on comedic timing. Then thrill to the *whoosh* of water from the amazing twin gushing geysers! Bow in the presence of the powerful palikoi! And be sure to fill out the customer satisfaction survey before you leave!

WATER, WATER, EVERYWHERE

by Pete the Palikos

Being a god of a local underground water supply, I'm naturally tapped in to the goings-on at Camp Half-Blood. Exploding toilets? Heard about that one. Son of Poseidon claimed in a stream during capture the flag? Got the details courtesy of Zephyros Creek. Underwater kiss? Canoe Lake gushed about it for days afterward.

Stories like that trickle in to Paulie and me all the time. We've heard stuff that made us flush. I'd tell you more, but I don't want to flood you with information that might bog you down. But pay us a visit sometime if you want.

We'd come to you, but Chiron has banned us from the showers.

THE STRAWBERRY FIELDS

Brought to you by Pete the Palikos

Is there a tastier treat on a hot summer day than a plump, juicy, sun-warmed strawberry? Mouthwateringly delicious, you can't eat just one. Luckily, here at Camp Half-Blood, strawberries are always on the menu—and on the outbound delivery truck!

PICK YOUR OWN

by Miranda Gardiner

Unless you're a child of Demeter or Dionysus, you'll probably overlook the strawberry fields while you're at Camp Half-Blood. I get that. Unlike the combat arena, the climbing wall, Half-Blood Hill, and other common areas, the fields are ordinary—well, except for the whole growing-perfect-berries-year-round thing.

It's too bad if you overlook the place, though, because the strawberries play a vital role at camp. They make us money, which pays for a lot of useful stuff here at Camp Half-Blood. Think that complimentary orange T-shirt you're wearing just magically appeared out of nowhere? Not quite.

You might be interested in knowing how the decision to grow strawberries came about. Then again, you might not. Feel free to move on to the next chapter if you're not. Just know you'll be missing out on some truly delicious camp info.

Still with me? Okay, here's how it went down.

Back in ancient times, Camp Half-Blood was

self-sustaining—a bastion of locally grown produce and free-range meat and poultry products. When the camp moved to Long Island, though, the crops and herds didn't come with it. For a long while campers had to make do by hunting, fishing, and gathering, Old-World-caveman-style. What we couldn't hunt and gather, we traded for with local farmers, which was okay when Long Island was sparsely populated.

Then New York City ballooned into a megalopolis and urban sprawl oozed onto the island, with communities erupting nearby almost overnight. After the third mortal sighting of teenage demigods running through neighborhoods with bows and arrows, Chiron decided it was time to make some changes.

He convened the head counselors of the nine inhabited cabins to discuss the issue. (The Hephaestus kids were on a quest for Celestial bronze, and Zeus's cabin was empty because he'd curtailed his extracurricular activities to appease Hera. The Hunters were on a stopover, though, so Cabin Eight was occupied.)

"We need a way to supply the camp," Chiron said. "Any ideas?"

"Yes! We take what we need by force!" bellowed the leader of the Ares cabin.

"Or we could just, you know, steal it," suggested the Hermes representative.

"No, no!" The son of Apollo whipped out his lyre. "We should sing for our supper, as did the minstrels of yore!"

"Of your what?" asked the Dionysus counselor.

"What?"

" 'The minstrels of *your*,' " the Dionysus girl said impatiently. "Of your *what*?"

A representative of the visiting Hunters intervened. "Not *your*. *Yore*."

The Dionysus girl gave up.

"This is getting us nowhere." The daughter of Athena stood. "Chiron, the camp needs a steady source of income."

"Agreed," Chiron said. "Suggestions?"

"One." She rested her fingertips on the table and surveyed the others with great solemnity. "We will sell something that people will buy in massive quantities."

"Wine!" called the Dionysus girl.

"Weapons!" yelled the Ares boy.

"Vocal arrangements in four-part harmony!" sang out the Apollo counselor.

"Food."

All eyes turned to the Demeter boy who had

spoken. He shrugged. "People always need food. Big city like New York, lots of people—lots of customers."

Chiron stroked his beard. "I like it. But what kind of food?"

That wasn't an easy question to answer. The Athena and Dionysus cabins wanted to sell food associated with their godly parents: olives and olive oil in honor of Athena; and grapes, grape juice, grape jelly, and wine (again) for Dionysus. The Hermes, Artemis, and Ares kids suggested putting their herding, hunting, and slicing-and-dicing talents to use and opening a butcher shop. Poseidon's daughter campaigned loudly for a seafood shack that offered "both Manhattan *and* New England clam chowder." Apollo's son, still stuck on his original idea, tried to woo the Aphrodite counselor to his cause by pointing out that music was the food of love. She wasn't buying it—and neither, she said disdainfully, would any self-respecting customer.

The discussion was escalating into an argument when the Demeter head counselor offered one last suggestion. "What about this?" He held out a small red object.

"Miniature explosive!" the Ares boy bellowed. "Duck!"

"It's not an explosive or a duck," the Demeter boy said. "It's a berry native to this land. Grows all over the place here."

The Aphrodite girl wrinkled her nose. "Excuse me, but *ew*! There are seeds all over the outside! *So* unattractive. And *red*? That color is *so* overdone, fruit-wise."

"Yes, but it's tasty," the Demeter counselor said. "I call it a *strawberry*."

"Why?" the Athena girl wanted to know.

"Because blueberry, raspberry, blackberry, and cranberry were taken. Here, try one." He spilled a handful onto the table.

The other counselors and Chiron sampled the strawberries. *"Sweeeet,"* drawled the Dionysus counselor. Even the Aphrodite girl agreed—though she picked off the seeds first.

Chiron asked the Demeter boy to stand. "It seems we have our product," he said. "Will you and your siblings oversee the crop and grow it in abundance?"

The Demeter boy straightened his shoulders and lifted his chin. "We will make it our sacred duty," he said, "though we might ask the satyrs for backup on the reed pipe and the Dionysus kids for an assist now and then."

The Dionysus counselor gave him a thumbs-up.

The Apollo boy strummed his lyre for attention. "Gentle souls, hear my pledge! I will make it *my* sacred duty to name and market our newfound venture." He strummed another chord, adjusted the tuning, and strummed again. "I will even compose a catchy jingle to advertise our wares throughout the fair streets of New York. Like a plague, this jingle will infect the minds of everyone who hears it. Soon all the world will sing of our product. The jingle shall go a little something like this . . ."

Fortunately, the other counselors talked him down before he could create a virulent, incurable ear worm. But the Apollo campers *did* do a great job marketing the new product, obviously keeping secret the fact that our divine new food was, in fact, grown by semidivine beings.

And that, newbie demigods, is how the Delphi Strawberry Service came to be.

Hello? You still reading? Hello?

Shoot. I knew I should have worked in a fight scene.

DO I GET TO KEEP THE T-SHIRT?

And Other FAQs

Answered by Percy Jackson, Annabeth Chase, and Nico di Angelo

PJ: We're a little limited on time, so let's get right to the questions.

So, do I get to keep the T-shirt?

PJ: You do, but since clothes tend to get slashed, burned, and bloodied here, you might want to purchase additional ones at the camp store.

AC: Percy!

PJ: What? Oh. Guess that makes life here sound a little dangerous.

NDA: Deadly, even.

AC: Nico!

PJ and NDA: Anna-be-eth!

AC: Idiots.

PJ: You'll be fine here. Probably. It's when you go on a quest that you'll encounter . . . trouble.

A quest? Do I have to go on a quest?

AC: You may not believe it now, because this is all so new to you, but getting picked for a quest is every demigod's dream. It's what we train for. It's what we're born to do.

PJ: You might not get picked right away. I mean, sure, I did—I was here, what, less than a week before I headed out to face death?

AC: You were a special case, Seaweed Brain.

PJ: Aw, you called me special!

NdA: She also called you Seaweed Brain.

"Face death"? Am I going to die?

NdA: I'll take this one. Yes, you will die—someday. When you do, you'll go to live, er, to *exist* in the Underworld.

PJ: Leo didn't.

NdA: Leo cheated death with a potion that he shouldn't have had. Without it, he'd have stayed dead. Like he was *supposed* to.

PJ: Hazel came back too.

NdA: That's totally different! I brought her back on purpose.

PJ: Just saying that not everyone who dies stays dead.

NdA: Next question.

What if I don't like it here? Can I go home?

AC: I've never been homesick. I bet that feeling stinks. But before you pack your bags for home, ask yourself, who will protect you out there in the mortal world? Who will teach you to use your powers? Who will really understand what it's like to be a demigod?

PJ: You can always Iris-message home. I hear moms in particular like that.

Will my conversations be private, or does Iris stay on the line?

PJ: You know, I never thought about that.

AC: I'm sure Iris hits mute. Plus, these days she's too busy running Rainbow Organic Foods and Lifestyles—her new whole-foods, gluten-free, vegan business—to listen in.

NɒA: Gods, I'd rather be stuck in a bronze jar with only pomegranate death-trance seeds again than eat that ROFL stuff.

How long has Camp Half-Blood been here?

PJ: Oh, man, that's a toughie. Some date it to the 1860s—

AC: But George Washington was a demigod, so if *he* trained here, the American version of the camp could be a hundred years older. Wow, I'm going to have to research that.

NɒA: You newcomers could always ask your godly parents, but honestly, time is so different for the deities I bet he or she doesn't know, either.

Where was it before? I mean, after ancient Greece?

PJ: Um . . . Annabeth, you want to take this one?

AC: Well, there was Rome, obviously. After the fall of the empire, the camp kind of moved from country to country, depending on which one was the major power of the time. I'm not sure of the exact locations, actually. You'd have to ask Chiron.

PJ: Congrats, kid, you stumped a daughter of the Wise One!

Last question: Will I really get zapped by lightning if I call Zeus's Fist the "Poop Pile"?

PJ: Only one way to find out!

NᴅA: Go ahead, kid! I'm sure my dad would love to meet you.

AC: Percy! Nico!

PJ and NᴅA: Anna-be-eth!

AW, SUMMER'S OVER . . .

by Percy Jackson

Pavement, or the surface of a road, comes in many forms. There's your asphalt (pronounced *ass-fault*, not *asp-halt*), your cobblestone, your gravel, your concrete, your—

Ha! Gotcha! Bet you thought you'd lost the ability to see through the Mist, didn't you?

What . . . you mean you weren't fooled?

Meh. Okay, then. Back to being serious.

Outside of camp, the days are getting shorter, and the nights are getting cooler. Inside, campers are talking about classes they'll be taking back at their mortal schools. Summer's nearly over, and that means Camp Half-Blood will be closing. Right?

Wrong!

Camp Half-Blood remains open all year round for demigods who, for one reason or another, can't or don't want to go home. If you fall into that category, just be sure to inform whoever is in charge—Chiron, Mr. D, or maybe some other immortal—that you intend to stay. That way, the cleaning harpies won't eat you. Come to think of it, it might be a good idea to state your intentions in writing . . . just to be safe.

I've never stayed past summer, but I've visited a few times in the off-season. It's pretty nice around here then. Quiet, because only a dozen or so campers stick around. Sometimes the magical borders let in snow—the good, packable kind for making snowballs and snow sculptures. It's more relaxed, too, as if trouble has been put on hold. Even the monsters in the woods seem to calm down. (Whoops, did we forget to tell you about those? Our bad.)

From what I've heard, the off-season is a great time for demigods to work on pet projects. For instance, this winter Malcolm will begin weaving the Polias peplos for the Panathenaia (try saying that ten times fast!). Will and Nico hope to find a way to keep Nico from passing out after he shadow-travels. (Did we forget to tell you what that was? Ask Nico about it sometime. Or have him demonstrate—just be ready to catch him.) I suspect Miranda Gardiner and Sherman Yang will be doing many things together; I won't say more, out of respect for their privacy.

As for me, I'll be back home, eating my mom's blue food, going to school, and hanging out with

Annabeth. At least, that's my plan. I'd like to say I'm sticking with it. But because I'm a demigod, my plans seem to change rather unexpectedly.

You'll find that out soon enough. Because guess what?

You're a demigod too.

And now if you'll excuse me . . . someone's blasting on the conch horn outside. That can't be good. . . .

About the Campers (in Order of Appearance)

PERCY JACKSON—Son of Poseidon, god of the sea, and Sally Jackson. Wavy hair, sea-green eyes, wiry build. Can control water.

CHIRON—Immortal centaur. Son of the Titan Kronos and the nymph Philyra. Brown eyes, brown hair and beard, powerful white stallion body. Longtime trainer of demigods and current activities director of Camp Half-Blood.

ANNABETH CHASE—Daughter of Athena, goddess of wisdom and weaving, and Dr. Frederick Chase. Long hair, gray eyes. Superior strategist, outstanding architect, rescuer of the long-lost Athena Parthenos. Hero.

CONNOR STOLL—Son of Hermes, god of thievery, messages, and trickery (mortal parent unknown). Blue eyes, brown hair. Younger brother of Travis Stoll. Current head counselor of Cabin Eleven. Known for pranks.

VALENTINA DIAZ—Daughter of Aphrodite, goddess of love (mortal parent unknown). Very attractive.

RACHEL ELIZABETH DARE—Daughter of Mr. and Mrs. Dare (both mortals, first names unknown).

Red hair, green eyes. Can see the future. Current
Oracle of Delphi.

THALIA GRACE—Daughter of Zeus, god of the sky,
lightning, and thunder, and Beryl Grace. Half
sister of Roman demigod Jason Grace. Once
a pine tree, now immortal lieutenant of the
Hunters of Artemis. Spiky black hair, electric-blue
eyes. Extremely powerful, but afraid of heights.
Hero.

LEO VALDEZ—Son of Hephaestus, god of forges,
fire, and metalwork, and Esperanza Valdez.
Brown eyes, black hair, short stature, fidgety. Can
summon fire. Hero.

MALCOLM PACE—Son of Athena, goddess of wisdom
and weaving (mortal parent unknown). Gray eyes,
blond hair. Substitutes as head counselor of Cabin
Six when Annabeth Chase is off campus.

ELLIS WAKEFIELD—Son of Ares, god of war (mortal
parent unknown). Muscular.

LAUREL AND HOLLY VICTOR—Twin daughters
of Nike, goddess of victory (mortal parent
unknown). Competitive and athletic. Dark hair.

NYSSA BARRERA—Daughter of Hephaestus, god
of forges, fire, and metalwork (mortal parent

unknown). Brown hair. Shares duties as head
counselor of Cabin Nine with Jake Mason.

WOODROW—Satyr (half-goat, half-man). Instructor at
Camp Half-Blood.

PETE—A palikos, god of geysers. Off-white muddy
complexion, foamy hair, milky eyes. His bottom
half is steam; his top half is that of a muscular
humanoid.

MIRANDA GARDINER—Daughter of Demeter, goddess
of agriculture (mortal parent unknown). Green
eyes. Shares duties as head counselor of Cabin
Four with half sister Katie Gardner.

NICO DI ANGELO—Son of Hades, god of the
Underworld, and Maria di Angelo. Black hair,
black eyes, pale skin. Very powerful. Travels
regularly between camp and the Underworld.
First Greek demigod to learn of Camp Jupiter.

Also mentioned:

FREDERICK CHASE—Annabeth Chase's mortal father.

JULIA FEINGOLD—Daughter of Hermes, god of
thieves and messengers.

HARLEY—Son of Hephaestus, god of forges.

THE HUNTERS OF ARTEMIS—Girls who pledged
themselves to Artemis, goddess of the hunt,

and promised to remain celibate. Granted immortality.

SALLY JACKSON—Percy Jackson's mortal mother.

CLARISSE LA RUE—Daughter of Ares, god of war.

PAOLO MONTES—Son of Hebe, goddess of youth.

BILLIE NG—Daughter of Demeter, goddess of agriculture.

BUTCH WALKER—Son of Iris, goddess of rainbows.

SHERMAN YANG—Son of Ares, god of war.

And finally, the star of the show, an immortal who shines as bright as the sun because he *is* the sun, a god who needs no introduction, please give it up for . . . Apollo!

GLOSSARY

ACHILLES—the best fighter of the Greeks who besieged Troy in the Trojan War; extraordinarily strong, courageous, and loyal, he had only one weak spot: his heel

AENEAS—a Trojan hero, the son of Aphrodite and a favorite of Apollo; becomes king of the Trojan people

AMPHORA (AMPHORAE, pl.)—a tall ceramic jar

ANDROMEDA—the daughter of the Ethiopian king, Cepheus, and his wife, Cassiopeia; after Cassiopeia bragged that her daughter was more beautiful than the Nereids, Poseidon sent a sea monster, Cetus, to attack Ethiopia; Perseus saved Andromeda from the rock she was chained to as a sacrifice

APHRODITE—the Greek goddess of love and beauty; she was married to Hephaestus, but she loved Ares, the god of war

APOLLO—the Greek god of the sun, prophecy, music, and healing; the son of Zeus and Leto, and the twin of Artemis

ARCAS—the son of Zeus and Callisto, a nymph follower of Artemis; Zeus disguised himself as

Artemis in order to seduce Callisto; after Hera became jealous and transformed Callisto into a bear, Zeus hid their son, Arcas, in an area of Greece later called Arcadia

ARES—the Greek god of war; the son of Zeus and Hera, and half brother to Athena

ARGONAUTS—a band of heroes who sailed with Jason on the *Argo*, in search of the Golden Fleece

ARGUS—a hundred-eyed giant sent by Hera to guard a nymph named Io

ARTEMIS—the Greek goddess of the hunt and the moon; the daughter of Zeus and Leto, and the twin of Apollo

ASCLEPIUS—the Greek god of medicine; son of Apollo; his temple was the healing center of ancient Greece

ATALANTA—a Greek hero; the daughter of King Iasus, who left her on a mountaintop to die because he wanted a son; she grew up in the wilderness and eventually became one of Artemis's Hunters; she sailed with the Argonauts as the only woman among them

ATHENA—the Greek goddess of wisdom

ATHENA PARTHENOS—a giant statue of Athena; the most famous Greek statue of all time

ATHENA POLIAS—an olive-wood, life-size statue of
Athena Polias ("of the city") that was located in
the temple to Athena at the Acropolis of Athens,
Greece

CALLISTO—a nymph who had a son with Zeus
and was transformed into a bear by the jealous
Hera; Zeus later placed her into the sky as the
constellation Ursa Major, or "the Great Bear"

CASSIOPEIA—wife of the Ethiopian king Cepheus,
and mother of Andromeda; she angered Poseidon
when she claimed that Andromeda was more
beautiful than the Nereids

CELESTIAL BRONZE—a rare metal deadly to monsters

CENTAUR—a race of creatures that is half-human,
half-horse

CETUS—the sea monster Poseidon sent to attack
Ethiopia as punishment when Cassiopeia boasted
that her daughter, Andromeda, was more
beautiful than the Nereids; Andromeda was
sacrificed to the monster but ultimately saved by
Perseus

CHARMSPEAK—a blessing bestowed by Aphrodite
on her children that enables them to persuade
others with their voices

CHITON—a Greek garment; a sleeveless piece

of linen or wool secured at the shoulders by brooches and at the waist by a belt

CYCLOPS (CYCLOPES, pl.)—a member of a primordial race of giants, each with a single eye in the middle of his or her forehead

DEMETER—the Greek goddess of agriculture; a daughter of the Titans Rhea and Kronos

DIONYSUS—the Greek god of wine and revelry; a son of Zeus; activities director at Camp Half-Blood

DRAKON—a gigantic yellow-and-green serpentlike monster, with frills around its neck, reptilian eyes, and huge talons; it spits poison

DRYADS—tree nymphs

EIDOLON—a possessing spirit

ENCELADUS—a giant created by Gaea to specifically destroy the goddess Athena

GAEA—the Greek earth goddess; mother of Titans, giants, Cyclopes, and other monsters

GOLDEN FLEECE—this hide from a gold-haired winged ram was a symbol of authority and kingship; it was guarded by a dragon and fire-breathing bulls; Jason was tasked with obtaining it, resulting in an epic quest

GREEK FIRE—an incendiary weapon used in naval battles because it can continue burning in water

GROVE OF DODONA—the site of the oldest Greek
Oracle, second only to the Oracle of Delphi; the
rustling of trees in the grove provided answers to
priests and priestesses who journeyed to the site

HADES—the Greek god of death and riches; ruler of
the Underworld

HARPY—a winged female creature that snatches
things

HEBE—the Greek goddess of youth; daughter of
Zeus and Hera

HECATE—goddess of magic and crossroads; controls
the Mist

HEPHAESTUS—the Greek god of fire and crafts and
of blacksmiths; the son of Zeus and Hera, and
married to Aphrodite

HERA—the Greek goddess of marriage; Zeus's wife
and sister

HERMES—the Greek god of travelers; guide to the
spirits of the dead; god of communication

HESTIA—the Greek goddess of the hearth

HIMATION—an outer garment worn by the ancient
Greeks over the left shoulder and under the right

HUNDRED-EYED—Argus was a hundred-eyed giant
sent by Hera to guard Io, a nymph with whom
Zeus was involved

HUNTERS OF ARTEMIS—a group of maidens loyal to
    Artemis and gifted with hunting skills and eternal
    youth as long as they reject men for life
HYPNOS—the Greek god of sleep
IO—a nymph who attracted Zeus's attention and was
    guarded by a hundred-eyed giant named Argus
IRIS—the Greek goddess of the rainbow, and a
    messenger of the gods
JASON—a Greek hero; the leader of the Argonauts'
    expedition in the quest of retrieving the Golden
    Fleece
KOPIS—a three-foot-long sword with a forward-
    curving blade
KRONOS—the youngest of the twelve Titans; the
    son of Ouranos and Gaea; the father of Zeus; he
    killed his father at his mother's bidding; Titan
    lord of fate, harvest, justice, and time
LABYRINTH—an underground maze originally built
    on the island of Crete by the craftsman Daedalus
    to hold the Minotaur
LYRE—a string instrument, similar to a small harp,
    used in ancient Greece
MANTICORE—a creature with a human head, a lion's
    body, and a scorpion's tail
MINOTAUR—the half-man, half-bull son of King

Minos of Crete; the Minotaur was kept in the
Labyrinth, where he killed people who were sent
in; he was finally defeated by Theseus

MIST—a magic force that disguises things from
mortals

MOUNT OLYMPUS—home of the Twelve Olympians

MOUNT PELION—a mountain in the southeastern
part of Thessaly in central Greece; the homeland
of Chiron the centaur, tutor of many ancient
Greek heroes

MYCENAE—the capital city that Perseus and
Andromeda founded

MYRMEKE—a giant antlike creature that poisons
and paralyzes its prey before eating it; known for
protecting various metals, particularly gold

NAIAD—a water nymph

NEMEAN LION—a lion that ravaged the area of
Nemea; its fur was impervious to human weapons;
slain by Heracles

NEMESIS—the Greek goddess of revenge

NEREIDS—water nymphs

NIKE—the Greek goddess of strength, speed, and
victory

NYMPH—a female deity who animates nature

OMPHALUS—stone used to mark the center—or navel—of the world

ORACLE OF DELPHI—a speaker of the prophecies of Apollo

OURANOS—the Greek personification of the sky; father of the Titans

PALAESTRA—the Greek goddess of wrestling

PALIKOI (PALIKOS, sing.)—twin sons of Zeus and Thaleia; the gods of geysers and thermal springs

PANATHENAIA—an ancient religious festival in Athens; the Athenians went in procession to the Acropolis, sacrificed one hundred oxen, and gave offerings, including a richly embroidered cloth, to the goddess Athena in the Parthenon temple

PARTY PONIES—groups of centaurs that are wild and drink root beer; known for attaching boxing gloves to the tips of their arrows and using paintball guns with Celestial bronze dust mixed into the paint

PEGASUS (PEGASI, pl.)—a winged divine horse, sired by Poseidon, in his role as horse-god

PEPLOS—an outer robe or shawl worn by women in ancient Greece, hanging in loose folds and sometimes drawn over the head

PERSEUS—a Greek hero; one of his many feats of
    bravery was rescuing Andromeda from the sea
    monster Cetus
POSEIDON—the Greek god of the sea and of horses;
    son of the Titans Kronos and Rhea, and brother
    of Zeus and Hades
PYTHON—a monstrous serpent that Gaea appointed
    to guard the Oracle at Delphi
RIVER STYX—the river that forms the boundary
    between earth and the Underworld
SATYR—a Greek forest god, part goat and part man
SHADOW-TRAVEL—a form of transportation that
    allows creatures of the Underworld and children
    of Hades to use shadows to leap to any desired
    place on earth or in the Underworld, although it
    makes the user extremely fatigued
STROPHION—a garment worn by females in ancient
    Greece; a soft band placed underneath the breasts
    to give them support
TARTARUS—lowest part of the Underworld
TITAN WAR—the epic ten-year battle between the
    Titans and the Olympians that resulted in the
    Olympians taking the throne
TITANS—a race of powerful Greek deities,
    descendants of Gaea and Ouranos, that ruled

during the Golden Age and were overthrown by a race of younger gods, the Olympians

TROJAN—of Troy

TROJAN WAR—According to legend, the Trojan War was waged against the city of Troy by the Achaeans (Greeks) after Paris of Troy took Helen from her husband, Menelaus, king of Sparta

TROY—a city situated in modern-day Turkey; site of the Trojan War

TYCHE—the Greek goddess of good fortune; daughter of Hermes and Aphrodite

UNDERWORLD—the kingdom of the dead, where souls go for eternity; ruled by Hades

URSA MAJOR—the Great Bear, the constellation form of Callisto, whom Hera turned into a bear in a fit of jealousy and Zeus made eternal by making her a cluster of stars

URSA MINOR—the Little Bear, the constellation form of Arcas, Zeus's son with Callisto

ZEUS—the Greek god of the sky and the king of the gods

DON'T MISS THE LATEST PERCY JACKSON ADVENTURE!

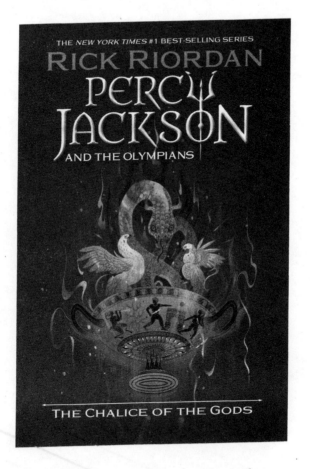

Turn the page for a sneak peek,
but beware of getting sucked in!

ONE

I GET FLUSHED

Look, I didn't want to be a high school senior.

I was hoping my dad could write me a note:

Dear Whoever,
Please excuse Percy Jackson from school forever and just give
him the diploma.
Thanks,
Poseidon

I figured I'd earned that much after battling gods and monsters since I was twelve years old. I'd saved the world . . . three times? Four? I've lost count. You don't need the details. I'm not sure *I* even remember them at this point.

Maybe you're thinking, *But wow! You're the son of a Greek god! That must be amazing!*

Honest truth? Most of the time, being a demigod blows chunks. Anybody who tells you different is trying to recruit you for a quest.

So there I was, stumbling down the hallway on my first morning of classes at a new high school—-again—-after losing my entire junior year because of magical amnesia (don't ask). My textbooks were spilling out of my arms, and I had no idea where to find my third-period English class. Matt and biology had already melted my brain. I wasn't sure how I was going to make it to the end of the day.

Then a voice crackled over the loudspeaker: *"Percy Jackson, please report to the counselor's office."*

At least none of the other students knew me yet. Nobody looked at me and laughed. I just turned, all casual like, and meandered back toward the administration wing.

Alternative High is housed in a former elementary school in Queens. That means kiddie-sized desks and no lockers, so you have to carry all your stuff from class to class. Down every hall, I could find cheery reminders of the school's former childhood—smudges of finger paint on the walls, unicorn stickers peeling off the fire extinguishers, the occasional ghostly whiff of fruit juice and graham crackers.

AHS takes anybody who needs to finish their high school career. It doesn't matter if you are coming back from juvie, or have severe learning differences, or happen to be a demigod with really bad luck. It is also the only school in the New York area that would admit me for my senior year and help me make up all the course credit I'd lost as a junior.

On the bright side, it has a swim team and an Olympic-sized pool (no idea why), so my stepdad, Paul

Blofis, thought it might be a good fit for me. I promised him I'd try.

I'd also promised my girlfriend, Annabeth. The plan was that I'd graduate on time so we could go to college together. I didn't want to disappoint her. The idea of her going off to California without me kept me up at night. . . .

I found the counselor's office in what must've once been the school infirmary. I deduced that from a painting on the wall of a sad purple frog with a thermometer in its mouth.

"Mr. Jackson! Come in!"

The guidance counselor came around her desk, ready to shake my hand. Then she realized I had six thousand pounds of textbooks in my arms.

"Oh, just put those down anywhere," she said. "Please, have a seat!"

She gestured to a blue plastic chair about a foot too low for me. Sitting in it, I was eye level with the jar of Jolly Ranchers on her desk.

"So!" The counselor beamed at me from her comfy-looking, adult-sized chair. Her bottle-thick glasses made her eyes swim. Her gray hair was curled into scalloped rows that reminded me of an oyster bed. "How are you settling in?"

"The chair's a little short."

"I mean at school."

"Well, I've only had two classes—"

"Have you started on your college applications?"

"I just got here."

"Exactly! We're already behind!"

I glanced at the purple frog, who looked as miserable as I felt. "Look, Ms.—"

"Call me Eudora," she said cheerfully. "Now, let's see what brochures we have."

She rummaged through her desk. "Poly Tech. BU. NYU. ASU. FU. No, no, no."

I wanted to stop her. My temples were throbbing. My ADHD was pinging around under my skin like billiard balls. I couldn't think about college today.

"Ma'am, I appreciate your help," I said. "But, really, I've kinda already got a plan. If I can just get through this year—"

"Yes, New Rome University," she said, still digging through her desk drawer. "But the mortal counselor doesn't seem to have a brochure."

My ears popped. I tasted salt water in the back of my throat. "The mortal counselor?"

My hand drifted toward the pocket of my jeans, where I kept my favorite weapon: a deadly ballpoint pen. This wouldn't have been the first time I'd had to defend myself from an attack at school. You'd be amazed how many teachers, administrators, and other school staff are monsters in disguise. Or maybe you *wouldn't* be amazed.

"Who are you?" I asked.

She sat up and smiled. "I told you. I'm Eudora."

I studied her more closely. Her curled hair *was* in fact a bed of oysters. Her dress shimmered like a jellyfish membrane.

It's weird how the Mist works. Even for demigods, who see supernatural stuff all the time, you have to concentrate to pierce the barrier between the human world and the godly one. Otherwise, the Mist just kind of plasters over what you see, making ogres look like pedestrians or a giant drakon look like the N train. (And believe me, it's embarrassing trying to board a drakon when one rampages into the Astoria Boulevard station.)

"What did you do with the regular counselor?" I asked.

Eudora waved her hand dismissively. "Oh, don't worry about her. She couldn't help you with New Rome. That's why *I'm* here!"

Something about her tone made me feel . . . not reassured, exactly, but at least not personally threatened. Maybe she only ate other guidance counselors.

Her presence felt familiar, too—the salty tingle in my nostrils, the pressure in my ears as if I were a thousand feet underwater. I realized I'd encountered someone like her before, when I was twelve years old, at the bottom of the Mississippi River.

"You're a sea spirit," I said. "A Nereid."

Eudora chuckled. "Yes, of course, Percy. Did you think I was a dryad?"

"So . . . my father sent you?"

She raised an eyebrow, as if she was starting to worry I might be a bit slow on the uptake. Weirdly, I get that look a lot.

"Yes, dear. Poseidon. Your father? My boss? Now, I'm

sorry I can't find a brochure, but I know you'll need all the usual human requirements for New Rome University: test scores, official transcripts, and an up-to-date psycho-educational evaluation. Those aren't a problem."

"They aren't?" After all I'd been through, it might've been too early to judge on that last one.

"But you'll also need a few, ah, special entry requirements."

The taste of salt water got sharper in my mouth. "What special requirements?"

"Has anyone talked to you about divine recommendation letters?" She looked like she really wanted the answer to be yes.

"No," I said.

She fiddled with her jar of Jolly Ranchers. "I see. Well. You'll need three letters. From three different gods. But I'm sure for a demigod of your talents—"

"*What?*"

Eudora flinched. "Or we could look at some backup schools. Ho-Ho-Kus Community College is very nice!"

"Are you *kidding* me?"

The Nereid's face started to glisten. Rivulets of salt water trickled from her oyster-bed hair.

I felt bad about getting angry. This wasn't her fault. I knew she was only trying to help me because my dad had ordered her to. Still, it wasn't the kind of news I wanted to deal with on a Monday morning. Or ever.

I steadied my breathing. "Sorry. It's just . . . I *need* to get into New Rome. I've done a lot of stuff for the gods over the years. Can't I just, like, e-mail them a recommendation form . . . ?"

Eudora's eyebrows knotted. Her dress was now sloughing off sheets of seawater. A pool of it spread across the green-tile floor, seeping ever closer to my textbooks.

I sighed. "Ugh. I have to do *new* quests, don't I?"

"Well, dear, the college admissions process is always challenging, but I'm here to help—"

"How about this?" I said. "If *my father* really wants to help, maybe he should explain this to me himself, rather than sending you here to break the bad news."

"Oh. Well, that would be, um—"

"Out of character," I agreed.

Something buzzed in Eudora's hairdo (shell-do?), making her jump. I wondered if maybe she'd gotten an electric eel stuck in her oyster bed, but then she plucked out one of the shells. "Excuse me. I have to take this."

She put the shell to her ear. "Hello? . . . Oh, yes, sir! I . . . Yes, I understand. Of course. Right away."

She set the shell on the desk and stared at it, as if afraid it might ring again.

"Dad?" I guessed.

She tried for a smile. The saltwater lake was still spreading across the office floor, soaking my textbooks, seeping through my shoes.

"He thinks you might be right," Eudora said. "He'll explain this to you in person."

She said *in person* the way most teachers say *in detention.*

I tried to act cool, like I had won an argument, but

my dad and I hadn't talked in . . . a while. He usually only brought me to his underwater palace when a war was about to start. I was hoping maybe he'd give me a week or so to settle in at school before he summoned me.

"Great. So . . . I can go back to class?"

"Oh, no, dear. He means *now*."

Around my feet, the water swirled into a whirlpool. The tiles began to crack and dissolve.

"But don't worry," Eudora promised. "We'll meet again!"

The floor dropped out from under my chair, and I plunged into a churning maelstrom with a thunderous *FLUSH!*

TWO

⚕

MY DAD HELPS OUT*
(*NO ACTUAL HELPING OCCURS)

You know you've been a demigod too long when you're flushed out of your school straight into the Atlantic Ocean and you're not even surprised.

I didn't try to fight the current. I could breathe underwater, so that wasn't an issue. I just sat in my blue plastic chair and rocketed through Poseidon's Private Plumbing System™, powered by a five-billion-gallon tsunami. Faster than you could say, *Well, that sucked*, I erupted from the seafloor like I'd been coughed up by a mollusk.

As the sand cloud around me settled, I tried to get my bearings. My nautical senses told me I was about forty miles southeast of the Long Island coast, two hundred feet down; no big deal for a son of Poseidon, but, kids, don't try this at home. A hundred yards in front of me, the continental shelf dropped into darkness. And right on the precipice stood a glittering palace: Poseidon's summer villa.

As usual, my dad was remodeling. I guess when you're immortal, you get tired of having the same crib for centuries. Poseidon always seemed to be gutting, renovating, or expanding. It helped that when it came to undersea building projects, he had pretty much infinite power and free labor.

A pair of blue whales was towing a marble column the size of an apartment building. Hammerhead sharks slathered grout between rows of coral brickwork with their fins and cephalofoils. Hundreds of merfolk darted here and there, all wearing bright yellow hard hats that matched their lamp-like eyes.

A couple of them waved at me as I swam through the worksite. A dolphin in a reflective safety vest gave me a high five.

I found my dad standing by a half-constructed infinity pool that looked over the abyss of the Hudson Canyon. I wasn't sure what the point of an infinity pool was when you were already underwater, but I knew better than to ask. My dad was pretty chill most of the time, but you didn't want to question his stylistic choices.

His clothes, for instance.

Some of the Greek gods I'd met liked to morph their appearance on a daily basis. They could do that, being, you know, gods. But Poseidon seemed to have settled on a look that worked for him, even if it didn't work for anyone else.

Today, he wore rumpled cargo shorts that matched his Crocs and socks. His camp shirt looked like it had been targeted in a paintball war between Team Purple and Team Hello Kitty. His fishing cap was fringed with spinnerbait lures. In his hand, a Celestial bronze trident thrummed with power, making the water boil around its wicked points.

With his athletic frame, dark trimmed beard, and curly salt-and-pepper hair, you'd think he was maybe forty-five—until he turned to smile at you. Then you noticed the weathered lines of his face, like a well-worn mountainside, and the deep melancholy green of his eyes, and you could appreciate that this guy was older than most nations—powerful, ancient, and weighed down by a lot more than water pressure.

"Percy," he said.

"Hey."

We have deep conversations like that.

His smile tightened. "How's the new school?"

I bit back the urge to point out that I'd only made it through two classes before getting flushed into the sea. "So far it's okay."

I must not have sounded convincing, because my dad furrowed his bushy eyebrows. I imagined storm clouds forming along the Atlantic coast, boats rocking in angry swells. "If it's not up to snuff, I'd be happy to send a tidal wave—"

"No, it's cool," I said hastily. "So, about these college rec letters . . ."

Poseidon sighed. "Yes. Eudora volunteered to counsel you. She's the Nereid of gifts from the sea, you understand. *Loves* helping people. But perhaps she should have waited a bit before breaking the news. . . ."

In other words: Now *he* had to do it, and he didn't like that.

If you've concluded that Poseidon is a "hands-off" type of parent, you win the chicken-dinner award. I didn't even meet him until I was in middle school, when (purely by coincidence) he needed something from me.

But we get along okay now. I know he loves me in his own way. It's just hard for gods to be close to their mortal offspring. We demigods don't live long compared to the gods. To them, we're sort of like gerbils. Gerbils who get killed a lot. Plus, Poseidon had a lot of other stuff going on: ruling the oceans; dealing with oil spills, hurricanes, and cranky sea monsters; remodeling his mansions.

"I just want to get into New Rome University," I said. "Isn't there any way you can . . . ?" I wriggled my fingers, trying to indicate godlike magic that could make problems disappear. Not that I'd ever seen such a thing. Gods are much better at magically creating problems than making them go away.

Poseidon combed his mustache with the tip of his trident. How he did that without cutting his face, I don't know.

"Unfortunately," he said, "those recommendation letters are the best I could do. They are the only way the Olympian Council will let you work off your debt."

Communicating underwater is complicated. I was partly translating his words from whale-song hums and clicks and partly hearing his voice telepathically in my head, so I wasn't sure I'd understood him.

"I haven't got any student debt," I said. "I haven't even been accepted yet."

"Not student debt," Poseidon said. "This is the debt you owe for . . . existing."

My heart sank. "You mean for being a child of one of the Big Three. *Your* kid."

Poseidon gazed into the distance, as if he'd just noticed something interesting in the abyss. I half expected him to shout, *Look, shiny!* and then disappear while my head was turned.

About seventy years ago, the Big Three gods—Zeus, Poseidon, and Hades—made a pact not to sire any more demigod children. We were too powerful and unpredictable. We tended to start major wars, instigate natural disasters, create bad sitcoms . . . whatever. Being gods, the Big Three still found ways to break the pact and not get in trouble. Instead, it was us demigod kids who suffered.

"I thought we'd moved past this," I muttered. "I helped you guys fight the Titans—"

"I know," my dad said.

"And Gaea and the giants."

"I know."

"And—"

"My son." The edge to his voice told me it would be best to stop listing my greatest hits. "If it were up to me, I would waive this ridiculous requirement altogether. Alas, someone"—he glanced up, *someone* being code for *my unreasonable brother Zeus*—"is a stickler for rules. You were never supposed to be born, so you are technically ineligible for New Rome University."

I couldn't believe this.

Also, I could *totally* believe this.

Just when I thought I might catch a break, I didn't. The Olympian gods seemed to think I was their personal kickball.

I relaxed my jaw to keep from grinding my teeth. "So, three recommendation letters."

Poseidon brightened. "Zeus wanted it to be twenty-five. I talked him down to three."

He looked like he was waiting for something.

"Thank you," I grumbled. "I don't suppose you could write one for me?"

"I'm your father. I would be biased."

"Yeah, we wouldn't want any bias."

"I'm glad you understand. To earn each letter, you will have to undertake a new quest. All three will have to be completed before the application deadline of the winter solstice. Each time a god writes you a letter of recommendation, give it to Eudora, and she'll put in your file."

I tried to think of gods who might cut me some slack and give me simple quests. I'd helped lots of immortals over the years. The trick was coming up with some who would *remember* I had helped them—or even just remembered my name. "I guess I can ask Hermes. And Artemis . . . ?"

"Oh, you can't go asking the gods. They'll have to come to you. But don't worry!" Poseidon looked really pleased with himself. "I took the liberty of putting your name on the Olympian quest board."

"The what now?"

Poseidon snapped his fingers and a neon-yellow flyer appeared in his hands. It was an ad with my photo and this copy:

PERCY JACKSON WILL DO YOUR QUESTS

(IN EXCHANGE FOR COLLEGE RECOMMENDATION LETTERS)

The bottom of the flyer was cut into little strips with my home address on each one.

The photo looked like it had been taken from inside my bathroom mirror, which raised a whole bunch of disturbing questions. My hair was wet. My eyes were half closed. A toothbrush was sticking out of my mouth.

"You already posted this, didn't you," I said.

"It wasn't a problem," Poseidon assured me. "I had my sea sprites put them up all over Mount Olympus, too."

"I am so . . ."

"Grateful." His hand settled heavily on my shoulder. "I know. I also know you weren't expecting this extra obstacle, but just think! Once you get into college, you should have a much easier life. Monsters hardly ever attack older demigods. You and your girlfriend . . ."

"Annabeth."

"Yes. You and Annabeth will be able to relax and enjoy yourselves."

Poseidon straightened. "And now I think I hear my interior designer calling. We still haven't decided whether the bathroom tile should be seafoam or aquamarine. Wonderful to see you again, Percy. Good luck with the quests!"

He thumped the base of his trident against the patio stones. The floor opened, and I was flushed right back through the ocean floor without even a plastic chair to sit in.

Other Books from the World of Percy Jackson

ABOUT THE AUTHOR

RICK RIORDAN, dubbed "storyteller of the gods" by *Publishers Weekly*, is the author of five #1 *New York Times* best-selling middle grade series with millions of copies sold throughout the world: Percy Jackson and the Olympians, the Heroes of Olympus, and the Trials of Apollo, based on Greek and Roman mythology; the Kane Chronicles, based on ancient Egyptian mythology; and Magnus Chase and the Gods of Asgard, based on Norse mythology. Rick cowrote and produced an eight-episode series based on the first Percy Jackson book, *The Lightning Thief*, for Disney+. He is also the publisher of an imprint at Disney Hyperion, Rick Riordan Presents, dedicated to finding other authors of highly entertaining fiction based on world cultures and mythologies. His most recent novels are *The Sun and the Star: A Nico di Angelo Adventure*, an instant #1 *New York Times* best seller that he cowrote with award-winning author Mark Oshiro, and *Percy Jackson and the Olympians: The Chalice of the Gods*. Rick lives in Boston, Massachusetts, with his wife and two sons. Follow his news at RickRiordan.com.